HERMITS DIE ON THURSDAY

There is a cold clarity to the world of *Hermits Die on Thursday*, as if each story were etched into a slab of mountain quartz and left to hum under moonlight. At times Gregory Ariail's characters—plague saints, fungus queens—emerge familiarly from Appalachia. At other times they seem to rise up from the old, slow-ticking cosmos where grief is currency and time runs crooked. Reading this book, I kept asking: what century am I in? What species? And does it even matter? These stories bend genre and undo history, tilting the reader into surreal terrains where a goat might fuse with a cliffside or a plague might carry not death, but mercy. These stories are funny. They're also reverent—toward the land, the body, and the stubborn human hope that persists in the face of silence. Ariail has written a book that feels ancient and freshly struck all at once.

—Grey Wolfe LaJoie, author of *Little Ones*

These stories feel like they were found on the underside of a rock that's probably never been moved in a remote part of the world, the old world, the world underneath our own that we forgot the name of a hundred years ago. I approach them with caution, myself. They changed me. Read them slowly and at your own risk.

—Ander Monson, author of *Predator: A Memoir, a Movie, an Obsession*

From Appalachia to medieval England, clear across the North Atlantic to Iceland, Gregory Ariail's *Hermits Die on Thursday* explores solitude and mysticism. Gleaming brilliantly at its surrealist edges, Ariail's short story collection stupefies and delights, reimagining the hermit myth, turning it upside down, and making it his own.

—Robert Gwaltney, award-winning author of *The Cicada Tree*

HERMITS DIE ON THURSDAY

Stories of Appalachia and the Dark Ages

Gregory Ariail

Illustrations by
James Hutton and *Aleksandra Apocalisse*

MERCER UNIVERSITY PRESS
Macon, Georgia

MUP/ P721

Published by Mercer University Press
1501 Mercer University Drive
Macon, Georgia 31207

29 28 27 26 25 5 4 3 2 1

Books published by Mercer University Press are printed on acid-free paper that meets the requirements of the American National Standard for Information Sciences—Permanence of Paper for Printed Library Materials.

Printed and bound in the United States.

This book is set in Adobe Caslon.

Cover/jacket design by Burt&Burt.

ISBN 978-0-88146-977-6 (Print)
978-0-88146-978-3 (eBook)

Cataloging-in-Publication Data is available from the Library of Congress

"Queen Elizabeth as Fungus" first appeared in *The Golden Key* (2018); "All Hermits Died on Thursday" in *The Southeast Review* (2019); "Transubstantiation" in *Indiana Review* (2019); "The Hog Drive" in *Animal* (2018); and "Eljay's Exile" in *DIAGRAM* (2014).

CONTENTS

I

APPALACHIAN APOCRYPHA

Queen Elizabeth as Fungus

Queen Elizabeth still exists in the Appalachian Mountains.

Old man Volney took me down to Devil's Elbow where a cascade froths against a corner of the mountain. The river there is rapid, deep, and dangerous even for trout.

"We gotta dive down," he said, tying his long white beard around his neck so that it wouldn't catch on anything underwater. He stripped down to his underclothes.

"Can't go entirely naked before the queen," he said.

I followed his lead, minus the beard-tying, and stripped down to my underclothes.

"The current will suck us right down under the cliff and spit us out on the other side."

"And that's where she is?"

"In a clearing just above it. A pretty ol' place. Now jump in exactly where I do."

He vanished into the river. I took a big breath and was pulled through the water like blood through a vein. In no time I was thrown above the surface. Spikes of sunlight danced high above me. Spluttering, I got my bearings. The old man stood on the first step of a rock staircase leading out of the grotto. I swam over to him, and he hauled me up with a lumberjack's strength.

Up the staircase we went, hugging the wall on the narrow steps. Above it was a forest of Appalachian hardwoods that gave way to an acre of luminous greenery without trees.

Something was in its center, like an assembly of gemstones blunted and faded with age.

"Is that a mushroom patch?" I asked.

Old man Volney pressed a finger to his lips.

I walked behind him. The shapes and colors came into focus and my heart skipped a beat.

The old man kneeled. Before us were a thousand mushrooms and mycelium webs that formed, very roughly, the shape of the great queen I'd seen in old portraits. Her gown was made of honey fungus and turkey tails. The gills of wooly milkcap formed the intricate pleats of her neck ruff. Sickly-white hoof fungus sprang up in a loose oval that resembled a human face. Tracing the upper arc of this face were a few scarlet cups that indicated thinning red hair.

And yet lying in the moss and dirt was a necklace of very real pearls.

A voice from the earth commanded: "Kneel."

I kneeled.

"Have you been to England?" the voice asked sadly. "Have you seen the tors of Dartmoor, the silver Isis, the cathedrals where choirs sing matins and vespers to move the soul?"

"I have," I said.

"Have you been to the barren North? Helvellyn, Blenchathra. Those eternal rocks swathed in snow and browning ferns, not a single tree in sight. Have you seen them?"

"I have," I said.

"And do you not miss them with all your heart?"

I could not say no to a queen, or that England had broken me, so I simply shook my head.

"Just like the others," she said. "England isn't your home. Nor, I assume, are these mountains. I thank my stars I will never be your queen. It is a burden to rule those who will never find a home."

Old man Volney kissed the mushroom that formed the farthest corner of her gown. He stood up.

"Come on," he said. "You're not the feller I hoped you were. You're no bard fit for a queen. She's like leaves in the woods and won't last long. At this point you're just wasting our time."

I followed him back into the forest. There he brushed aside some pine needles and opened a door in the ground.

"That'll lead you out," he said. "I'm sorry to say it's nowhere near where we came in."

"You're not coming with me?"

"Can't do it."

For the last time I saw his dark eyes, white beard, and gourd-colored skin.

I passed through the door. On the other side was an ocean. I was far from Appalachia, far from my family and friends. This journey had gone so far awry that it could never be fixed. I needed someone to help me. But before I went searching for a kind soul I plopped down on the sand and looked out at the ocean. I threw shells into the waves. It was so ugly I wanted to cry.

All Hermits Died on Thursday

The six hermits of the Nantahala region of North Carolina died mysteriously yesterday. On this day, March 20th, 1899, the town elders had planned to gather the hermits together for the first time to beg their collective advice on the planned railroad and various omens of the new century.

Beard of the Ages

March 21.—The hermit of Granite City, Hoyle Thompson, choked to death on his own beard on Thursday. Mr. Buell Mae found him in his cave, at the back of the boulder field, and proceeded to pull it from the old timer's mouth. According to Mr. Mae, it took three hours to extract the entire beard from the hermit's clenched teeth. The coroner measured the beard at 25.8 feet long, the longest ever recorded in North Carolina. Hoyle was 89 years of age. The hermit left the following note addressed to the inquisitive, dated Midnight, March 20, 1899:

> In three hours I shall be gone, feasted to death on my own magnificent beard, the pride of my life. I'll ride the moon all the way down to hell to meet my mother and Mr. Price, my Latin teacher. Bad bowels are the cause; a phantom knife in my bladder that twists deeper each time I inhale. No one knows of my troubles. It's my fault that no one knows or cares, but I couldn't be other than I am. I've loved this valley and these rocks. They've protected me from thieves, well-wishers, and the law. Do what

> you will with my carcass. Grind it, mince it, flatten it, plant a tree in it, sell it for meat, give it to science, parade it through town, cradle it, shit on it. I'm in pain, desperate pain, and I'm canny enough to know when to make an appointment with the wind.

Last Cherokee in Nantahala

March 21.—Transylvania County, whose borders lie near this town, has claimed for many years the only Cherokee hermit in Nantahala, in the person of James Cuttawa. Those who attempted to parley with him on Jocassee Mountain were met with a strange sight—the hermit hovering upside down, his legs splayed, his white hair touching the floor. This affrighted those coming to inquire about his health and the veins of gold reported to fill the caves beneath his cabin.

When the writer of this column opened Mr. Cuttawa's door to beg his attendance at the hermit council, he was met with a similar sight. The hermit, clothed in deer skins, hovering upside down, his hair a white waterfall, and a string of frozen saliva running from his mouth to the floor. No pulse was detected. The writer searched for a means by which Mr. Cuttawa was suspended in the air but located none. On the boards near his head were etched or burnt these puzzling words: "Those strong footholds. Why did they place them beyond me?"

Turkey Herder

March 21.—Dame Nature provided Imogene Bascom with all she needed. She lived for forty-nine years in the hollow of a great American chestnut tree, to which she affixed a door on rope hinges. She was well-known in the vicinity of Ellicott Rock for her herd of turkeys that numbered two dozen or more. She drove them about here and there and they flitted to the treetops whenever a thunderstorm was about to break. Reputedly, ten turkeys drowned over the years, so hypnotized were they by the storm that they gazed up at the falling rain, opening their beaks with amazement, forgetting to close them even as they brimmed with water.

A natural historian might catalogue the following curious facts about Ms. Bascom:

> Hair: white as snow. Beard: only on her neck. Birthplace: Wales. Diet: berries, nuts, and sassafras tea. Favorite pastime: licking the rocks around her tree and the items within her tree in order to keep everything clean. Clothes: the same raccoon skins for forty-nine years. Literacy: Wordsworth during the day and the Bible at night. Slept on: turkey feathers and leaves, usually on her stomach. In this position she was found dead. The turkcys gathered in a circle around her tree, their heads bowed. Today they were rounded up by Mr. Willoughby to be plucked.

389-Year-Old Spaniard

March 21.—Doctor Beardsley Drake, a gentleman famous for physick, philosophy, and his lust for curiosities, set out Thursday to meet the wonderful old hermit of Bearwallow Falls, aged 389 years. Soon his spyglass revealed the hermit, bathing in nothing but God's clothing in a pool beneath the remote waterfall. In a strange accent the hermit welcomed

Dr. Drake and led him along a narrow ledge behind the roaring water to his haunt. The cave was exceedingly damp with spray. The hermit's beard resembled a giant fox tail coiled around a leather belt.

The hermit pointed out a bit of rusty armor at the back of his cave, which he claimed he wore in the days of Hernando de Soto, when the Spaniard sought a fortune of gold in Western North Carolina. He recalled how he had crossed the Little Tennessee River with that great conquistador, found that its waters flowed westward, and concluded that the New World was much vaster than anyone supposed (it was he, a young though brilliant soldier, who had first elaborated this idea to de Soto). In his strange accent the hermit lamented how he had been left behind in a small fort to protect the Spanish interest, learn the native language, and convert the Cherokee to Christianity—all with a promise that de Soto would one day return, which he never did.

The hermit drank nothing but water from Bearwallow Falls. Dr. Drake, in search of more detailed information and desiring to study the hermit's teeth, loins, and forehead more closely, plied him with whiskey. Upon the first gulp of liquor, the hermit fell into spasms, foamed like a dog, and died.

Astronomer No More

March 21.—For thirty-nine years Anson Ham lived alone near the headwaters of the beautiful Tuckasegee River. He was an astronomer of no mean repute. Mr. Ham, a freedman, left the vicinity of Charleston after the War, seeking a space free of the mental and physical chains of the past, where he could pursue his research without threat or calumny. Mr. Ham maintained a twirling mustache rather than the customary beard of the Appalachian hermit.

Anson's house resembled a metal boat. It lay deep in a pine and hemlock forest, but in a great clearing in those woods, so that his lenses could pierce the night sky without obstruction. Scores of telescopes of different lengths poked out from his landlocked boat, like pins in a pin cushion. He hypothesized that Saturn's ring is not liquid, nor a single solid ring, but rather thousands of tiny ringlets made of particles of ice—a radical theory at odds with accepted science. He also hypothesized that there is a massive body, possibly a planet, beyond Neptune.

He catalogued his discoveries in a tome kept on his mantel. When I visited him on Tuesday, Mr. Ham appeared well and in good spirits until I casually took down his book of wonders to peruse its contents. Upon seeing me do this, a change came over his face. I did not ask permission to read it, yet my purpose was benign: a mere friendly interest. He snatched the book from my hand. He ripped out a page and ate it. He ripped out another page and ate it. I hastened from his abode. On Thursday Mr. Ham's body was found glutted with paper, his belly a massive balloon, ink leaking from his eyes—thus taking his discoveries with him to the grave.

The Ur-Hermit

March 21.—The impossible has occurred. Musidorus, the Ur-Hermit, this region's first creature—appearing before the Scotch-Irish, Germans, Spanish, Cherokee, panthers, bears, and foxes—has died. He did not occupy a particular mountaintop or valley, as many readers of this obituary doubtlessly know. He occupied *all* mountaintops in Nantahala. This is why some called him the All Hermit rather than Ur-Hermit, though those fondest of him simply called him Musidorus.

It was a familiar scene. Panting, with a stitch in your side, you finally crested a particular summit. Say that of Whiteside Mountain, Big or Little Green Mountain, Chinquapin or Satulah Mountain. You'd come across a sweeping view of the tangled knots of mountain, valley, hollow, and hill that distinguishes this corner of the world. If you felt the landscape deep in your bones your eyes might swim with tears—so many old memories, such intricate webs of flora, fauna, and rock; so much past and future. It was then, as the light refracted through the glaze of your tears, that you'd infallibly see Musidorus sitting on a warm bubble of sparkling rock, caught in a ray of light, even when the heavens dumped snow or at midnight—yes, even at midnight you would see that ray of honey-colored light break the darkness. And there he'd be. His beard pouring down the mountainside in waterfalls, the strands twirling around and grasping the distant hills like tentacles. He would sit in a full lotus posture, meditating, his hands resting in his lap, his thumbs lightly touching, breathing, simply breathing, the most placid expression on his face. His eyes would open just wide enough to see you. Slowly he would un-touch his thumbs and raise a palm; and just as you touched that palm, and the stars circled around your heart, he would vanish.

After the tragedy and ominous coincidence of the five human hermits dying on the same day, every journalist of the *Nantahala Herald* and every community member worth their salt sought the mountaintops at dusk to beseech Musidorus' council. Through our tears, we all saw the same thing. And we mourn this curse. Instead of a ray of light from outer space, and that peaceful ancient at its far end, barely touching the earth with his rump, there was something else: a gash in the air, viscera on the rocks, and tiny hairs spreading outwards like a beard detonated.

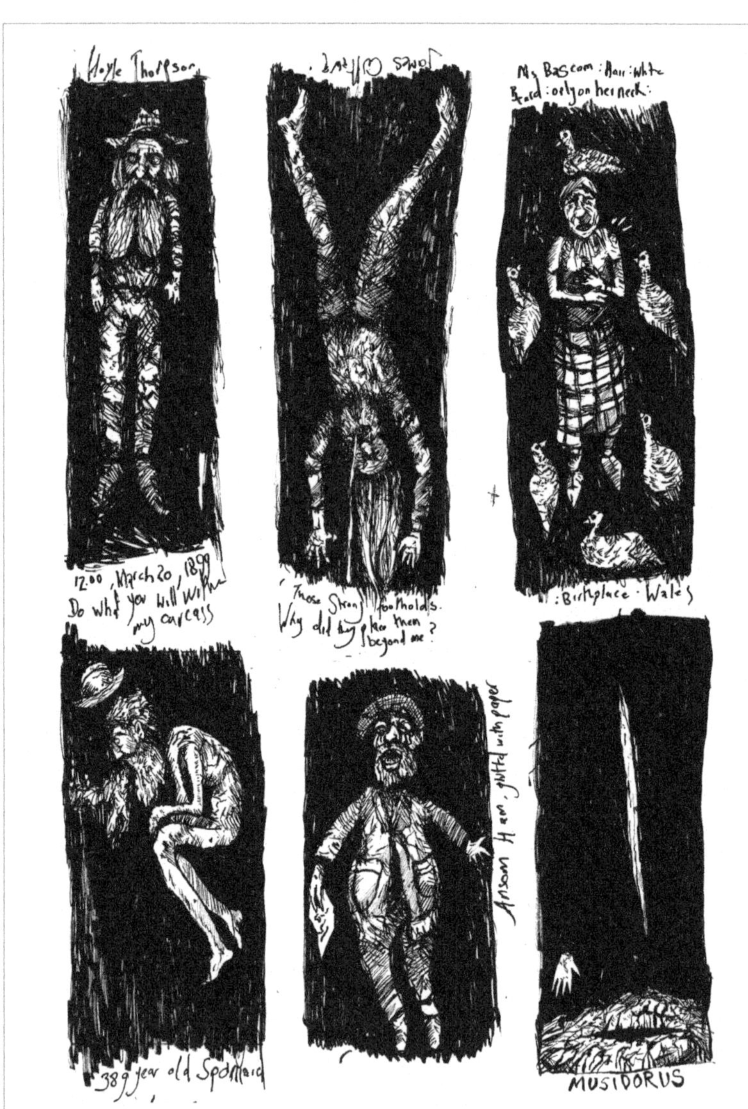
Hoyle Thompson
12:00, March 20, 1899
Do what you will with my carcass
Jones Clifford.
These strong footholds.
Why did they place them beyond me?
Ms Bascom : Hair : White
Beard : only on her neck :
: Birthplace · Wales
389 year old Spaniard
Anson Hem, glutted with paper
MUSIDORUS

The Hidden Mailbox

Gretchen crossed the dirt road and opened her mailbox. Junk mail galore. No package. Nothing special. Same old story. She nodded as if to say, *how could it be otherwise*?

Then something caught her eye—a scrap of metal in the dirt, tarnished like an old nickel.

She squatted down. She poked the hot metal and dug around it with her finger, expecting it to come loose. *Must be some pipe or building contraption*, she thought. The more she scratched around the object, the more surface was revealed. It was bigger than a cantaloupe, that was for sure.

Gretchen went back inside her house, threw the mail on the countertop, and searched the garage for a trowel. She'd need a tool to dig up the strange object. Her body thrilled at the prospect of what it could be but tried to manage her expectations; it was probably a piece of rubbish exposed by a recent storm. Yet it had to be fairly old. She'd moved into her house on her wedding day forty years ago and couldn't recall any construction work done near the mailbox.

Hardly anyone drove down her out-of-the-way mountain road; she would hear gravel popping under tires a quarter mile away, so she didn't worry about getting hit by a car as she dug.

Finally, after scraping away a few last layers of dirt, a curved capsule emerged. *Now imagine that. A mailbox under my mailbox*! It was warped, discolored, and clearly not very sturdy. This could be the mailbox of the family who had lived in her house in the fifties.

She pried open the door, telling herself it was empty and not to get her hopes up. But it wasn't empty. Inside, there was a thin stack of mail, including two packages.

She licked her lips. Life had just given her a chocolate chip cookie straight from the oven.

What was her surprise when, after shuffling through the items, she found that they were all addressed to her, Gretchen Felks. She gasped. First there was a twenty-year-old postcard from her daughter, a Buddhist monk in California who hardly ever called. It showed a temple with a golden roof submerged in forest and said on the back, "Love you, Mom. Not enlightened yet." Gretchen's heart hurt; she missed being close to her daughter.

Next was an envelope from 1998 from her best friend, Maple, who died three years back (well, former best friend—for the last decade or so they had talked less often since Gretchen had stopped reading as many books and listening to classical music). Inside was a ticket to a Bach concert in Asheville and a Happy Birthday note. Her friend had never mentioned this concert over the phone. Had Maple been offended? Had that been part of the reason their friendship eroded? *Ungrateful*, she heard Maple say. *Too selfish to trust.* Gretchen could hardly breathe.

How could these missives, years apart, occupy the secret mailbox? Was this some joke of the mailman's? She should complain to the post office. But no, they'd laugh her off the phone. No one would admit to burying a mailbox with a cache of old mail. They'd call her crazy.

She tore open one of the packages; she'd saved them for last. The paper was brittle, vintage one might say.

It was a book, an Everyman's Library edition of *Minor Poets of the Eighteenth Century*, which seemed like the most boring read imaginable. There was no return address, no note, and she could not imagine ordering it herself. Another joke, surely. Not a very funny one.

The last package was lighter. It turned out to be a video cassette tape—a VHS. She still owned a fair number of cassettes, but the grocery store hadn't sold them for decades.

A note taped to the cassette read: From Archibald.

Gretchen sat down.

She'd expected something from her ex-husband to materialize, not Archibald. This was a painful yet unnerving surprise. She didn't mind that an ant crawled into her sock. She chewed on a strand of hair.

Gretchen last spoke to Archibald on the phone forty-one years ago when she was in the courtship phase with her ex-husband. She had told Archibald never to call again but had secretly wanted him to. And he had called—just once. But she didn't respond when he spoke her name. She breathed into the phone for a few seconds and hung up. *Let him call one more time, and I'll talk to him*, she told herself. *He needs to prove how much he misses me*. But he never rang a second time.

She left everything in the road except the cassette and hurried inside. A VHS player sat atop her television and was partly hooked up, but it took fifteen tense minutes to find the missing cord. She'd never been good at that sort of thing and had never upgraded to a DVD player (mainly to annoy Maple, who called her a dinosaur). With her hands trembling, it took another few minutes to find the right channel.

Then the cassette was entered into the plastic mouth with a click and whir.

Her stomach dropped like she was on a carnival ride. Archibald's face peered out at her, exactly as it was in the early 1980s. Not the handsomest face. His forehead and eyes were a bit too small. Stray hairs poked from his nostrils. But his expression was genial, his hair thinning yet dark, and his lips full and gracefully cut. He'd loved hiking and finding waterfalls no one else knew about. She'd gone to school to be a librarian, and he a copyeditor, so they had plenty to discuss.

He smiled without showing his teeth. That was his way. Water crashed behind him.

She leaned closer to the screen.

"Gretchen," he said. Oh, that voice. A little wild, festive as a glass harmonica. "I'm here at Corncob River. I'm going to find the land beyond the gorge. We often talked about it and tried to make it past the giant boulder but failed. Today I won't fail to find that secret place. With this camera, I'll take you along with me. I won't speak much. I'm not trying to convince you of anything. I just want you to know that I can't ever forget you. And if I find a route to that place that none have ever seen on the North Carolina border, I promise to wait there for you. Not always, of course, but one day a year, the day of the summer solstice, when we hiked along Corncob River for the last time."

The screen fuzzed with static and wobbled iridescently, then panned over a waterfall's gushing tiers. The camera shook. He zoomed in on dark vortexes where leaves spun round and round, foaming cauldrons, natural rock sculptures, and darting salamanders. He zoomed out to show a boulder high as a castle gate, seemingly impassable: the place where, long ago, they'd been forced to stop. Nevertheless, they'd held each other and kissed at that dead-end, light as the mist floating up from the falls.

Archibald wedged his hand into a crack in the boulder. Gretchen scolded the television: "Don't go up there! It's not safe!"

The scene changed. He turned the camera to his dirty face. "I made it past the great boulder," he beamed. "Now to find where the river leaves North Carolina. The path is narrow and slippery, but I'll be fine."

Views of sandy beaches piled with driftwood. A band of mist, like a ragged slipper, gliding along clifftops immeasurably high. A splash. Water droplets on the lens, forking down. He'd fallen into the river! But next came a shot of fluorescent algae and a close-up of a thin white worm rotating, coiling and uncoiling, in a shallow pool. Then a shot of broad blue sky and the daytime moon.

Archibald covered the lens with his palm. The screen went black.

"I've found it," he whispered. His voice was distant and fuzzy as if water had damaged the microphone. Yet he expressed awe. "It's beyond anything," he continued. He got choked up. "If you could only be here. I promised never to come by your house, never to call again. I won't be faithful to you. I'm not a fool. I'll move on, mostly. But if you ever relent, meet me here on the summer solstice, next year or fifty years from now. It's the strangest thing imaginable." He laughed. "You won't believe what I'm seeing. But I won't show you the view unless you come...goodbye, Gretchen."

Light flared along the screen's rim, and the video ended with a wobble of color and ascending bars of static.

Gretchen rewound the tape and watched it again. And again. What day was it? What month? Mid-May. When was the summer solstice? Her mind spun. June. Over a month away. *Don't be an idiot*, she told herself. *This tape's from a million years ago*. And she'd found it in a buried mailbox. It was a trick. Some cruel soul was pulling her leg. She couldn't straighten out her thoughts. She wished she could call Maple for support. Even her daughter's infuriating mildness would be welcome, but the temple had no phone. She needed to talk it out and cool her nerves.

Even if she could be with Archibald in her old age, reconnect after all this time, would she want that? Realistically, how much had she thought about him before watching this video, before all those memories were reawakened and the flame rekindled? She dreamed about him now and then and woke with a distant ache, but regret hadn't consumed her days. Was there not freedom in her loneliness?

She'd never needed a partner. Marriage had been a lukewarm experience. Her daughter had left for good right when she'd turned eighteen. Her family life felt like an unfinished puzzle with pieces on the floor.

Was it Archibald's wild cry across the river that troubled her heart, or had this video merely interrupted her boredom? Had dissatisfaction with the present pulled her into the past?

A blaring noise. She jumped, expecting an attack from an intruder. But it was only the telephone, mounted on the kitchen wall. She ran over and picked it up. Probably a sales call or someone trying to hack her bank account.

"Hello?" she gasped.

Silence. Then static. The sound of rushing water? A scrambled voice spitting the same sounds over and over. A rumble of thunder or a boulder falling. Then the word "Gretchen," she could swear, spoken into a receiver muffled with moss. She imagined a phone, decrepit and falling apart, wooled over with moss. The mental image was as clear as a postcard picture.

Then came the dial tone's mournful note. He'd hung up.

Now Gretchen was frightened. Something was wrong. She felt a storm growing inside her, clouds flickering. Should she jump in her beat-up Cadillac, the car she'd bought as a retiree's private joke (the quintessential senior mobile)? Was Archibald in danger? Was she going insane? Before she could decide, she'd backed out of the driveway. She swung down the mountain, took the bypass to avoid town, and jerked the wheel left and right, left and right, squealing down the switchbacks to the hollow where Corncob River lay beyond a forest service road.

The dirt road had enough bumps and potholes to ruin her car, and she drove so fast that she almost wrecked it. Her undercarriage scraped. Gravel snapped against the windshield and cracked the glass.

Finally, the pull-off came into view, but no vehicle was parked there. No Ford pickup, Archibald's old truck. She laughed aloud, tears in her eyes. This was the only place to park—the area was too steep and rugged. And it wasn't even midsummer yet. What had she expected to find? Some evidence of his existence, a token that he still waited for her one day a year?

Gretchen opened the car door and breathed in the fragrant river wind. Perhaps she could find where the great boulder nearly corked the river. She could recreate Archibald's journey to the North Carolina border. Or at least go halfway. She hadn't hiked in years. Trees wavered and masses of white mountain laurel blurred. It was a resonant spot, no doubt about it.

She imagined Archibald outside a ramshackle hut, two miles upriver, holding a telephone connected to a wire he'd unspooled across the wilderness, gazing out at an unimaginable view, a miracle on the state line. Her mind a-whir, not knowing what she was doing or what she expected, she started down the trail. She passed Corncob Crook, where a cliff jumped from the water and forced the river to bend at a ninety-degree angle, sending it into a narrow, tumultuous chute. Archibald loved that spot. They had once fallen asleep there under the stars, soothed by the river's thunder, a memory lost until that moment. She half-believed he'd crawl out of the foam. "He's no merman," she said to herself. "Get it together."

Suddenly the water rose. The rapids roared and churned as from some distant storm. The natural wells and rock sculptures, shaped by the river for a hundred thousand years, vanished underwater.

Gretchen quickened her pace, and her knees began to ache. At last she reached the boulder where the trail ended. It leaned over her like a troll turned to stone. She looked around wildly.

"Archibald!" she cried. "Archibald! How far's the secret view?"

Water spread white lacework over the boulder; soon the river would inundate it.

"I can't climb the rock," she said. "It's too high and slick."

A phone rang. Not her phone. She didn't own a cellular device. A phone in the rock. It vibrated a little, otherwise she wouldn't have found it since it was overgrown with reindeer moss.

Gretchen picked up the handset and said breathlessly, "I'm here where the trail ends. Is that you? The river's rising fast. I don't have long before I'll need to go uphill. Tell me what to do."

"Gretchen?" The voice was shaky yet musical. Festive. Layered with time. Archibald's.

"It's good to hear your voice," she cried over the din.

The phone smelled like his mouth. She kissed the receiver, and the wet reindeer moss gave like lips.

"My love," he said. "If you could go back in time, would you have chosen me?"

She faltered. Why hadn't he simply said that he'd missed her? There was no time for such nonsense. "What does that matter? I'm here now. Hurry. How do I get to you?"

"Why did it take so long?" He sounded hurt. "It's not my time to wait at the state line. And the view's always cloudy in May. You're a month early and forty years late."

Archibald liked to scold. She suddenly remembered that. It had been a sticking point between them. When upset, he would lecture her without looking her in the eyes.

The phone hissed as he said more. A sheet of water fluttered over the boulder.

"Directions..." she thought she heard him say. "A shortcut..."

The current pulled at her feet and her heart went cold.

"I have to go!" she cried.

Gretchen dropped the phone; it scraped lifelessly on the rock. She didn't notice the path along the cliff etched in sunlight, level and broad as a bridge. She sped uphill in the other direction.

Even in his dreams, she ran away from him.

Transubstantiation

The poor farmer opened his door. He rubbed his eyes. There was a bank of snow a hundred yards in front of him, as well as to the left and right. Not banks, no—walls, three infinitely high walls of snow rising and rising until they framed the dawn moon.

He ran to the back of his house to see if there was an escape route through the snow, an opening to the south. The hope that had risen in his chest cracked like a boot heel on ice. The snow wall was there, too. His entire farm was imprisoned inside four walls of snow. Even if an avalanche had rushed from north, south, east, and west, how could it have stopped on the property line of his farm, frozen in a perfect rectangle?

He walked across the field in a daze. He opened the chicken coop and the four chickens, his only animals, escaped. After a minute or so of staring into the blackness of his own mind he realized this, gave a start, and snatched at a hen who beat her wings in a swift burst and slipped through his fingers. He chased the four chickens to take his mind off the white, glittering miracle around him.

Finally, his hand closed on the neck of a hen. His eyes widened in astonishment. She was the same feathery, stinky, writhing thing from the neck down to her reptile feet. But her head was a tiny human head, no bigger than a walnut. The face had a scraggly beard, bloodshot blue eyes, and luminous skin dripping with blood—the blood issuing from a tiny crown of thorns.

The other three chickens had the same face. Or nearly the same face. Atop their amber and white bodies sat little Christ heads, but with small variations between them. One chicken had a chiaroscuro face, the mouth a dark gaping hole amid sunlit skin. Another had wounds and barbs etched into its face; the beard was reddish, the brow furrowed, the eyes closed in inconceivable pain. The other's eyeballs gazed up at the heavens, never looking down, the beard dripping saliva, the purple tongue pouring over the lips like wine.

No words issued from the little Christ heads. Just clucks, moans, and squawks.

❧

The snow walls didn't go away. The grass withered. The dandelions withered. There was nothing to feed the miraculously changed chickens, no fodder to be gotten anywhere on the moribund farm. They ate and drank snow. He let the chickens roost in his house. Each day he cleaned up their runny and insubstantial shit.

The chickens were becoming ragged. They clucked and complained, huddled in his empty bookshelf. Their histrionic expressions never changed.

A time came when the farmer was starving, too. He felt the nagging, mystifying cramps of desperate hunger. Rashes formed on his tongue. Oftentimes he stood up only to fall down; the world blurred and sharpened in quick oscillations. He ate nothing but snow, carving out pockets from the snow wall with his hand and swallowing the icy grains until he was sick and cold.

There was no choice but to slaughter the chickens. The first one went into the slip knot. Knife in hand, he massaged the feathers around its neck. The chicken with its half-parted Christ mouth gobbled with curiosity and fear. The farmer slit its jugular. It flapped its wings as the muscles contracted and the blood drained out. He then severed the head, casting it on the ground, doing his best not to look into its face.

One by one the chickens were butchered. The four little Christ heads lay scattered below the slaughter table. The farmer ate big meals that made his bones burn with a desire to keep living. Very soon there was no chicken meat left.

The farmer hunched over, trembling. He prayed to God. Because it made sense to. He prayed to his dead mother, to his ex-wife, to the daughters he'd wanted but never had, to all the chickens in the world, to the hairs on his forearms. Deliver me from this miracle, deliver me, my loving friends, whom I've neglected all my life.

Nothing happened.

He found himself sidling up to the blood-smeared slaughter table, bending down, picking up a half-rotten, discarded Christ head. The snow reeled around him like the roving mind of God. Look at its face. Look at its face. The cheek flesh stripped away. The teeth protruding from a tangle of beard where the thin skin just below the lips had decomposed into a kind of cobweb.

Edibles remained, however. The meat of tongue. The milk of glazed eyes. The collapsed berry of a mole.

The farmer crunched through sour skin into the bone and ate everything, even the beard. He ate the second head.

The third. The fourth. Ravenously, unable to stop this access of need.

With each Christ head he consumed, the snow wall dropped by a quarter in height. The sun washed over the farm. The mountains, after the third head was eaten, showed their brown weave on the horizon. After the last head, the world opened to him again, the world like stained glass.

How could he not weep? Sweet freedom. But it was then that his bowels stirred. Something was wrong inside him. He dropped his trousers and scat erupted with a violence he'd never known. With an ancient violence. And when it was all over, and he was panting on the ground, his rump in the air, all four limbs on the dirt like the mammal he was, he saw inside his own scat the half-digested eyes, the brittle beards, and the crowns of thorns bright with new blood.

The Hog Drive

The most memorable words in the language aren't as beautiful as the things themselves: wood sorrel, geranium, October bean, Cherokee purple tomato, cushaw squash, bronze fennel. I observe my garden with a mother's eye, holding my belly in my hands. Oh son that will not have time to grow.

It's not mist sinking down the mountains this June morning but an ocean of hogs. They pour down like a line of latitude descending, inescapable, muddy, the mythical Okefenokee released.

Husband dead of a stroke at thirty. Cousin after the horror drank herself to death. Father still alive somewhere but has never been any help. Mother, whether alive or dead, belongs to the past.

The earth thunders. The drivers yell: "Sooey! Sooey!" The hog-wave thickens.

I'm trampled, picked up, bouncing on the backs of hogs, who, when aware of me, do their best to keep me afloat and not let me sink under their hooves. Their flesh radiates scarlet heat.

My garden, refuge of sweat and blood, where I came to pray when my husband died and my son began to flourish inside me—gone. Trampled into a waste of mud without a single memorial weed.

I'm carried towards the slaughter fields of Georgia. I recognize the mountains of my husband's kin. The granite cliffs like frozen mirrors. The pine trees orange with age and disease.

If I had a sermon to give, it'd be: find a hardworking mate. Don't despair if all you own is a garden. If you annoy people at first, keep annoying them, and they'll eventually love you.

At resting points, I thrust my head into the troughs with the rest of the hogs. The fodder we eat isn't the kind that'll keep you strong all day. Just corn stalks, potato skins, and rotting hay. When they're finished eating, the hogs lick my swollen belly with warm geographic tongues.

We depart when the earth cools off. I get no rest on their jolting, shifting backs as they stampede into the night. The lashes of the whips never touch me thanks to their guardianship.

Many days. Days and days. Past scorched foothills, muddy rivers, bonfires, moonshine stills, and cotton fields. My son hasn't moved inside me for too long. My life is fully submerged in darkness.

☙

A plateau fattens the horizon. Atop it are black crucifixes. I sense that it's the endpoint. The hogs and I are driven up the plateau's sides. Crumbling clay sweeps downward as we climb towards the sky.

Healthy men await us at the top. Thousands. The entire male population of the Piedmont must be on this plateau. They stare at us with lascivious eyes, removing hammers and nails from their pockets. With my swollen belly and mud-caked skin they mistake me for a hog. They grab me by the arms and legs, hoisting me up to a cross and pinning me at the point where the beams intersect. Nails are driven through my shinbones and wrists. They do the same thing to all the hogs.

One hog, a wise elder, screams "sooey, sooey," so that the men gather below the cross it's suspended on. They whisper to each other, impressed. "That's a keeper," says one man to another. They extract nails from the hindlimbs that are twined together and the two forelimbs stretched apart.

The other hogs in the vicinity imitate it, screaming "sooey," hoping to have the same luck. But the men are only impressed with the initiator. The freed hog trots around and rubs against them. It doesn't lash out in vengeance. It stands on its bloody hind legs like an acolyte.

No longer do the hogs have any thought of me. They open their eyes only to close them.

Butcher parties come with weapons. Scythes, cleavers, and rusty swords. I cannot bear the cascading slop of organs. I cannot bear to see those bodies destroyed. I want to reach out a hand to them but can't.

When the butchers arrive at my cross, I stammer so unintelligibly that they still don't know me for a woman. My swollen belly proves enticing. They begin there, making a curved incision, despite my wild squirms and cries so shrill that the eyes of the angels dilate.

"What a paunch!"

"Pork belly for a year!"

"We got ourselves a screamer!"

Out spills an unformed human face. The butchers haul it out of me, stretching the umbilical cord that is no umbilical cord but a beard. No little limbs. No breathing nose or mouth. No ears to hear the sounds I've saved up inside me. Just a slab of jelly with two eyes and a beard.

"Bury my son," I cry, the tongue's spell broken.

Now the butchers understand their mistake. They gaze at me with new eyes. Sad eyes. They grip their overalls. They walk in circles. "A woman!" they yell to each other across the plateau.

They weep for me and my son but not for the leavings of the hogs nailed to crosses as far as the eye can see.

They want to take me down, but I don't let them. That's over with. At my command, they use their weapons to dig a hole at the foot of the cross. The face of my son is covered with red clay.

"Plant a garden where he lies," I say. "With heirloom seeds." And they do. A raised circular mound, a three sisters garden, seeded with white flour corn, October beans, and cushaw squash.

They kiss my feet, those dried legumes. I'm not who they think I am. I'm not a miracle. Nonetheless I tell them a final story—about a son so huge he can pick up his mother with one hoof.

Rubezahl

We prayed for fall to come but King Autumn didn't answer. Before long, we'd eaten all the summer crops. The valleys were littered with corn stubble and there wasn't a single blueberry to be found on the high ridges. We'd replanted the May vegetables, yet none had germinated. It should have been nearly winter. We ached for pumpkins and apples and crisp, dewy lettuces.

King Autumn had abandoned our little world for reasons unknown to us. Had we offended him somehow? Not praised him enough? We would have sent emissaries to distant lands for aid or council, but we were hemmed in on all sides by the great Tallulah Gorge, with its sheer cliffs ten thousand feet deep. The river had eaten around us until our lands became an island in the sky.

Every year King Autumn had blown in on his friend, the North Wind, and emptied his jug of red-gold ale over the land; the harvest unfurled, and everything wilted richly. Now the two friends were imprisoned somewhere or had quit their sacred duties. The pale sky was a windless waste.

Though the naïve may desire summer without end, with heat lying on them like a heavy blanket, the reality of such an event is a horror. The eternal cycles were broken. We chewed on thick, sour, nutrition-less leaves. The moonlight lathered us briefly before the sun oppressed us again.

Then my grandfather, his sleep inspired by hunger, perhaps, had a dream. A green man in jade-flecked armor with a moss-colored beard appeared and told him to deliver the following message to the villagers:

I am the spirit of Rubezahl. For autumn to be rekindled, you must collect all the art in your village, made by young and old, and pile it in the bog at dusk. The rest I'll do. But beware: don't be stingy. No matter how much the art means to you, cast it into the bog.

The next morning, in the meeting barn, the villagers reacted to my grandfather's dream.

"Who is Rubezahl?"

"Never heard of him."

"It's not wise to trust dream people."

"We don't have much art here."

"I don't want to burn my story about the giant and the fairy!"

"Or my painting of the North Wind."

"Well, what have we to lose?" I chimed in. "Maybe a bit of sacrifice, a bit of house-cleaning, so to speak, will do the trick. The old religions were all about sacrifice. If nothing happens, at least we'll have less clutter and clearer minds, and then we can devise a new plan to coax King Autumn back."

More than anything, I wanted to support my grandfather in public. We bickered a lot, but underneath it all were deep reservoirs of respect and love.

ᘓ

My grandfather, tall and wiry, looked as if he was carved from a walking stick; his beard reminded me of a mass of white creek foam. He was my only relative. My parents had died trying to build the bridge across the gorge, which now lay in ruins, only spanning ten feet of the gulf.

"Why didn't you tell me about this dream before telling everyone?" I asked.

"I've got to run everything by you, then," he said, "oh my wise granddaughter less than twenty years old? I wasn't aware of that. Thank you for letting me know."

"Stop it. You don't usually put much stock in dreams."

"This one was different. I woke up with a mission, a calling. It was a message from the other side of the gorge, that I'm sure of. The vision of the green man, that Rubezahl, has twisted me up inside."

"Just because it comes from the other side of the gorge doesn't mean it's true."

"It's more than that," he grumbled.

"And you're not cracked?" I asked. "You're completely sane?"

"I've always been as cracked as the rocks, you know that."

"Be serious."

"I swear to you, Winnow, this was no mere dream. It rang truc."

"And you believe it all? Why would tossing art into a bog make any difference to King Autumn?"

He raised his eyebrows, shrugged, and then began rummaging around the cabin for noteworthy objects.

ca

What constituted a work of art? The village contained plenty of part-time artisans (the rest of the time they farmed and foraged). The cobbler certainly made some lovely shoes tied with maple-red wool. Some of the broom maker's brooms were especially strong and the bristles scratched like old leaves in a gale. The potter sculpted faces into his mugs. And no one built better chimneys than me. I always chose the most curious, difficult-to-place stones, and my flues drew beautifully.

I couldn't knock down the chimneys I'd built and cart them up to the bog on Bee Green Mountain before nightfall. But would my chimneys even count?

My grandfather, sweating profusely, was bent over a few old paintings, probably done by my mother. I didn't have the heart to go over there and look. The pain was still too near, a specter always at my back.

I looked under my bed. There was a sheaf of birch paper on which were preliminary sketches of my chimneys, notations and measurements, and fanciful doodles of chimneys that could never exist: cloud-penetrating chimneys, snowy mountains balancing on chimney tops, a chimney growing from a woman's back—that sort of thing. Some of these drawings were new, others a decade old. I didn't have much, but those sheaves seemed the best 'art' I could offer Rubezahl.

I glanced at my grandfather. He was filling a basket, mainly with my mother's things.

I couldn't take it anymore. How could he dispose of his own daughter's work?

"Put them back," I snapped. "Surely the green man doesn't want those."

"But they're beautiful," he said with a tear in his eye.

I wanted to slap that tear clean off; it infuriated me. He saw the venom in my look.

"So we should give up the only hope we have?" he cried. "It's a fool's hope, yes, but I trust in it. *Don't be stingy*, the green man said. *No matter how much the art means to you, cast it into the bog.*"

"You're senile," I said and stormed out of the cabin into the burning, windless day.

☙

In the end, after an hour of peering across the gorge with my telescope and seeing nothing but dark green trees, as usual, I returned to the cabin to find my grandfather loading the cart. Gazing at distant cliffs and the faraway, mysterious mainland tended to put my mind at ease and things in perspective. I approached him with a conciliatory expression, and he noticed it right away.

"I don't like this any more than you do, Miss Chimbley," he said, using an old nickname for me.

I saw three paintings of my mother's on broad plates of pine bark: one a portrait of my birdlike father, another a landscape of a bridge arcing over a vast chasm, and the last a scene of fairies dancing in the woods, but the faeries' bodies were made from my milk teeth and their wings from maple seeds. I hadn't looked at these since my parents' deaths seven years ago.

It hurt. I missed my parents so much. But these objects weren't part of them anymore. Keeping them wouldn't heal the pain.

"Too bad your father was a minimalist, or we'd have more to offer Rubezahl."

My grandfather glanced away from me, anticipating some barbed words.

I threw my sheaves of chimney illustrations into the cart and rested my hand on his shoulder.

"Let's go," I said. "The sun's nearly set, and we have to haul this cart a mile uphill."

He squeezed my hand, and off we went. I hoped this scheme would work against all odds. It didn't seem likely. And I didn't want my grandfather to become a fool in the villagers' eyes. He was a good man.

☙

Atop Bee Green Mountain, the villagers encircled the bog. The dusk was grey as a meteorite. Everyone was solemn-faced. Doubt plagued our minds, as well as a newfound and ferocious possessiveness for things we didn't even know we valued. Children held dolls and little books of stories that they'd written or received, bound with string. A venerable old woman stood by a cartload of wooden figures she'd carved with great attention to detail. Gorgeously cut and woven gowns were bundled up in arms. A fiddle hung limply from a young man's hand. Written plainly before all were each other's inner lives, usually secreted away. Before the bog all were vulnerable.

With my eyes nearly shut, I began the procedure. I couldn't bear it any longer. I dumped my mother's paintings and my sketches and grandfather's ancient rings into the mud. In a frenzy, as if I'd shouted a battle cry, everyone followed suit; even the children seemed possessed by some demon of relinquishment. Carts were upturned, bundles were tossed like stones in a competition.

Soon hundreds of objects stuck out from the weedy muck. It was a kind of ritual garbage heap, and once the frenzy had passed, most of us, I could tell, felt a bit silly and considered wading into the bog to retrieve our treasures. A few unpleasant villagers winked at my grandfather. A group of youths bent together and whispered. Bitter laughs erupted here and there.

Suddenly, in a great wave, birds exploded from the treetops and flew away. Small mammals screeched and dashed from their burrows and hollows. For a moment I could have sworn that a white-tailed deer, a mythical creature not seen for hundreds of years, rose from the shadows, shook its antlers, and trotted deeper into the woods.

Everyone went silent. The atmosphere around the bog trembled.

Something was going on. I tried to focus my eyes in the dying light.

A man clad in green armor, half transparent in the dusk, was appearing in the center of the bog, our artworks peppered around him. He had a long, wild beard, like moss and lichen intertwined. It looked as though leaves had been stuffed into his eye sockets. He lifted his arms, and a green fire sprung up. The entire bog went up in flames. Our precious artworks glowed, popped, and sizzled.

With curious speed, the items started to collapse. I had the urge to leap into the muck and collect the charred wood of my mother's paintings, but awe kept me in check. Because the great miracle was just then happening: golden ash billowed into the trees; our handiwork turned to dust and washed the landscape in glitter. Some people's work produced more golden ash than others. My sketches emitted a handful, maybe, and my mother's paintings a few wheelbarrows' worth. The amount of it didn't correspond to the size of the work, but, maybe, to the care that went into it.

It took me a few minutes to realize that leaves were falling—red and brown and yellow leaves, curled and desiccated. A cool wind tumbled through the trees and pinecones slapped against the ground. We shivered despite the flames. It was a shiver of ecstasy. Knotty, bruised apples rolled across our feet. The green man in the bog showed no expression, except perhaps a slight frown. He kept his arms raised to the rising moon, but his arms seemed heavy and in pain.

As the golden ash plumed, the trees and plants aged and ripened before our eyes; we forgot the art and our covetousness, and wept. We clasped our hands and thanked this spirit, Rubezahl, who did not seem to want our thanks. In fact, the more we praised him, the more his frown hardened. Yet we couldn't help it. He had stepped into the land of dreams and saved us from ruin and confusion. He had replaced King Autumn.

The flames died and the green man stood amid the smoking bog. He lowered his arms and said, "Your art has helped me spark the harvest, but only for this year. Your farms and orchards have been temporarily healed but, as you will discover, their yield will be small, the fruits and gourds miniature. To have a richer harvest, you must make better and more beautiful things. If you devote yourselves, ardently, to the expression of your secret lives, maybe next autumn I can work stronger magic. For King Autumn is lost. I cannot find him anywhere. Never again, it seems, will autumn come unworked for, without sacrifice. Only with spiritual tinder can I bring about the harvest. In the meantime, don't worship me. I only come because all others have departed."

Very slowly, he faded into the night, and before we knew it, we were all stranded in the dark. No one had thought to bring a lantern, and our candles wouldn't light in the strong wind. So, hand in hand we wound our way down the cool, crackling mountain under the moonlight. It took many hours, but no one complained; the villagers chatted excitedly about the things they'd create in the coming year. My grandfather and I laughed and, without awkwardness, exchanged memories of my parents.

Eljay's Exile

The goat's head protruded from the mountain wall, the granite encircling its neck. Its body, if it had any at all, was trapped inside the rock.

Eljay leaned a ladder against the cliff. After he had climbed about thirty feet, the goat's horizontal pupils came into view. It looked at Eljay with weary eyes. There were no more questions in those eyes. Its grey hair was ragged and thinning.

The goat had lost the ability or the will to open its mouth for nourishment. Therefore, Eljay pushed a stout twig up one of its nostrils. When he did this, the goat's eyes looked less weary. Eljay could sense that it was in pain. But like a rusty trap, its mouth opened little by little.

A gourd hung around Eljay's neck. He tilted the gourd to the goat's mouth. The animal drank as much as it could, coughing when the flow was too strong. Most of the water ran down its beard.

Did the water pass into a body? Or into the cliff? Eljay had often probed the area where the goat's neck met the rock, searching for a dividing point between flesh and stone, but he had found none. Its coarse hair seemed to merge into the cliff seamlessly.

Perhaps he was missing something. The goat always seemed refreshed by the water he gave it, implying the presence of a body behind the rock. Had the animal wandered into a cave and, seeking sunlight and air, thrust its head into a small vent in the mountainside? What other explanation could there be? But something told Eljay this was not true. The goat, he knew, would die very soon.

ଓ

Eljay had much to regret. There had been fires. He had ruined crops and caused famine. When a friend was maimed, he had become disoriented in the forest and alerted others too late. Exile was a just punishment, he thought, for his mistakes. No one wanted him to suffer. To secure him against privation, the townspeople had loaded a sturdy wooden cart with supplies. This cart had given him endless trouble, but he could not have survived without it.

Since late summer, Eljay had lived in a shack on the summit of the mountain. He had not intended, as he passed through unknown lands, to stop and live on this mountain. He had intended to accomplish nothing but distance all the years of his life. But one day, as he lowered the cart handles and sat with his back to the wall of a cliff, thinking over the past, he saw the head of a goat protruding from the rock above him.

At first he could not believe his eyes. He climbed a tree to get a better look. When the goat noticed Eljay, his feet wedged high up in the fork of a trunk, it snorted and spat at him. Many times he was pelted with saliva. The animal swung its head back and forth until it panted from fatigue.

Eljay found it impossible to leave. Here was something that altered the known patterns of the world. Here, too, was an opportunity for him to change his ways. He would become the goat's benefactor and companion. The animal was, after all, solitary like him. And despite the absence of people in these lands, someone was bound to pass by the mountain at some point. Whoever it was would marvel at what he had found and inevitably ask him to come away with them to some faraway town.

For two weeks he built a ladder, which required all his ingenuity. Though it turned out to be more durable than the shack he had built, it was still barely adequate. The frame, forty feet high, listed as he ascended it for the first time, scraping against the cliff. A rung cracked under his foot.

By slow degrees, the goat began to desire Eljay's presence. In the afternoons, if he had not visited it or brought it food, it yowled, sending echoes across the valley. When autumn came, though, the animal suddenly stopped eating. It dipped its face into his palm but would keep its mouth shut. The fat beneath its fur dwindled. It would only drink water when forced. Eljay could not discover the reason for this change. He wondered how the goat had survived before he found it. He despaired because he wanted someone to see, before the animal died, that it relied on him.

☙

The signs of winter were beginning to show. Leaves floated in the air. The cliff, like a frozen waterfall, dropped vertically from the sky.

Eljay gripped a hammer in his hand. He could waste no more time. The creeks had flowed with slush that morning. Frost had collected in the goat's fur. No matter what he did, its mouth would not open anymore. The twig had no effect. A white crust had formed over the animal's lips.

The only option left to him was to try to free the goat from its prison in the rock. He dreaded the act. What if the mountain were indeed part of its flesh? Would extricating the animal from the rock cause it pain, or perhaps end its life? But he could waste no more time.

The hammerhead struck the granite and sparked. The goat's head lunged forward. Grains of mica split from the rock, whizzing past. The goat twisted its head toward Eljay, trembling. Its pupils sprang into dilation. If only it could open its mouth. For the second time the iron rebounded. What looked like urine leaked from the goat's nostrils.

Eljay went at it until his arm was numb and smoke issued from the cliff. He had made no progress. The rock would not fracture like the stones he had found decaying in the woods. The cliff was impenetrable. He dropped the hammer. He looked down at the goat, which hung its head, unconscious.

ଓ

A bearded man stood on the summit of a neighboring mountain. In a gloved hand he held the carcass of a squirrel. The trap, which would not be set again until next year, diminished in the distance as the man walked along the ridgeline. He had cut a path along this ridge long ago.

The wind blew over him as he descended the mountain, carrying the scent of smoke. He stood still for a moment and scanned the landscape. Beyond the trees he detected movement on the summit of a mountain to the northwest. In his two decades of trapping in this region, he had never encountered another soul.

If this were someone pursuing game, he wanted to meet them. The cliff of the mountain was not climbable, so he aimed for its sloping side. The summit, he guessed, could not be more than an hour's journey.

As the man approached the mountain's base, the sky grayed. The clouds were hardly visible when he passed the last trees and the bald summit opened before him like a meadow. He spotted Eljay sitting beside a woodpile that had lost its flame. Behind him was a shack of interwoven branches.

The man called a greeting. Eljay leapt to his feet. If there had been woods close by, he would have fled to them. He feared that this man would somehow do him harm. Then he remembered what he had been wanting all this time. He tried to calm himself by thinking of the goat.

The stranger came forward. He wore an outfit made of deerskins sewn together. His beard was like a board lifted from the dirt. He was dark-skinned and had alert blue eyes. He said that his name was Olmsted.

"Are you trapping hereabout?" he asked.

"No, I'm not trapping," Eljay said.

Something about the man's manner put him at ease. It was abrupt but not hostile.

Olmsted asked what he was doing in these mountains—he had never met anyone here before.

Eljay could not speak about his exile to the stranger. He did not want the man to scorn him. For a moment he hesitated. But as he met Olmsted's gaze, he recovered enough to say, "I left home in search of a marvel. I found one here, on this mountain. If you're willing, I'll take you to see it."

Olmsted disliked this strange, evasive talk. Something was not right with Eljay. He was old-looking, yet his voice was that of a man of thirty. The rags he wore stank of mildew and perspiration.

"Tell me what you mean by marvel," Olmsted said. "I've got a hundred traps to check before the snow arrives. I thought to meet someone of information up here. Otherwise, I wouldn't have bothered."

Eljay was on the verge of tears.

"There's a goat," he said. "I've been taking care of it since the summer. What you won't believe is that it's wedged into the cliff down there. It looks as if it's grown out of the rock. I know that's not what's happened," he added nervously, seeing that Olmsted's beard twitched, as if the man had bitten his lip in anger. "The thing is, something's wrong with the animal and I don't know what to do. I don't understand any of it. I need help or advice or anything you can give."

Olmsted was interested. A goat in this region, hundreds of miles from any town? Before he turned to trapping, he had kept a flock of goats. But they, like all the animals in the west, had died from the pox or dysentery. He had not seen a goat in years.

The man considered his options. The ridges in the west were darkening. Journeying back to his cabin at this hour was not worth the trouble. A goat pelt would get him a set of metal traps in town.

"All right," Olmsted said. "We'll leave first thing tomorrow."

He sat down and started kindling the fire Eljay had abandoned.

ℴℛ

Dawn revealed the bones of a squirrel in the firepit. The two men crawled out of the shack. Both were shivering. Olmsted started a fire to ward off the cold.

"Why didn't you take more time building that thing?" Olmsted asked, looking at the shack. He was almost in awe of its inadequacy.

"I didn't know any other way," Eljay said.

After eating a breakfast of mast, they followed a well-worn path down the mountain. Eventually they reached flat ground where the cliff rose, curving out of sight. Forty feet above them the goat's head hung from the rock. Its eyes were overgrown with lichen but its nostrils sniffed the air.

Olmsted heard a noise and looked up. He stood there, gripping his beard as if it were blown by a wind. "That's not possible," he said. He turned to Eljay and gave him a hard look. He had expected the goat to be at the cliff's base. Eljay withdrew the ladder from the leaves and leaned it against the mountain. He was flushed with anticipation. "I can't tell you what's happened," he said.

The man spat on the ground and wasted no time. Hand over hand, he began the ascent. He knew that Eljay had built the ladder, so he took extra care. The goat, sensing the approach of a stranger, bucked with a whine in its throat. At one point it knocked its head against the ladder, which tipped precariously. "Damn you," Olmsted cried as the ladder righted. When he reached the goat, he seized its horns; the animal blasted air through its nostrils but could not move anymore.

"Hold the ladder for me," he called down to Eljay.

Olmsted kept one hand on the goat's left horn and hooked his free arm around its neck. He pulled and strained until a rim of blood emerged on the rock around the animal's neck.

Eljay did everything in his power to stay quiet while Olmsted attempted to free the goat. His thoughts were in a fury of protestation. This was not the scenario he had imagined. If the man would not praise him for the discovery, he could at least be gentle with the animal Eljay had grown to regard as part of himself. Such a man, he thought, could never sympathize with his troubles.

After deciding that the goat was indeed anchored into the cliff, Olmsted continued to explore the animal with his hands. He pinched its withered pelt and shook his head. He pressed his ear to its neck, listening for a heartbeat. When a few minutes had passed, he rapped the granite with his knuckles.

"What can we do to help it?" Eljay called, his eyes glancing up the cliff. Olmsted stood against a sky of slow-moving clouds, inspecting the goat's horns. For some time the man did not reply.

"Not a thing," he said at last. "It doesn't have long to live. I've seen this disease before—must be the kidneys. But we'll get it out of the cliff, one way or another. I've got to understand how this happened."

☙

"I've designed a thousand traps in my day," Olmsted said. He talked while sawing a pine tree. "But that mountain's the best trap I've ever seen. Whether it's natural or someone carved a hole in it, I can't say. But the way the rock pinches down on that animal's neck, snaring it but not suffocating it—I could've never imagined such a thing. There's no doubt there's a body behind the rock. It's just a matter of getting to it the right way."

Olmsted and Eljay were building a lean-to in the forest a few yards from the cliff. The man would not spend another night among the disorder and exposure of Eljay's mountaintop home. He disliked Eljay less now that his story had proven true. He insisted that they remain in each other's company while they dealt with the goat.

That night the two sat talking over a fire.

"Don't you think there's a possibility," Eljay said, "that once the goat's out of the rock, it might recover and live?"

"Look," Olmsted said, "keeping that animal alive all this time, giving it water it doesn't want—it would've been better to leave it be. The only question is how it got up there in the first place."

"There must be something we can do," Eljay said in an unsteady voice. "It's the only thing I've ever taken charge of. I can't let it die."

Olmsted looked at Eljay through the smoke. "It's not for you to decide," he said.

With the fire still burning, and his eyes closed, Olmsted devised a plan. Back at his trapping cabin—one of many spread over five hundred miles—he had a set of tools that were more suitable than the ones Eljay had used: a chisel, a rope, a bellows, a mallet, and a set of buckets. Tomorrow he would go to his cabin and return with them. Alive or not, he would get the animal out of the rock in two days, no less.

☙

From afar, five points of flame could be seen on the cliff. They formed a pentagon in the night. Earlier, Olmsted had bored holes into the rock, an inch from the animal's neck. He had filled the holes with charcoal. By standing atop the ladder and working a bellows, he kept the embers burning. His object was to heat the stone surrounding the goat's neck until it scorched. At the critical moment, which was close at hand, Eljay would send up buckets of cold water by way of a pulley system Olmsted had devised. After the cliff was doused with enough water, the rock would fracture. This would either loosen the mountain's hold on the goat or, with luck, free it completely.

As he pumped the bellows at the ladder's top, Olmsted noticed Eljay was missing. He wiped his perspiring face. He cursed and looked at the goat, whose agony was so deep it was silent.

Eljay came back into the atmosphere of light carrying a bundle of blankets.

"What the hell are you doing?" Olmsted yelled. He gave a few pumps at the bellows. "Don't you move from those buckets again. The rock's hot as a furnace. It'll be ready any time now." He paused. "What are you spreading out those blankets for?"

"I don't want it falling to its death when the rock breaks up," Eljay said.

"That won't do any good," Olmsted yelled down to him. "If it falls forty feet, blankets won't save it."

Eljay distrusted the man's judgment but could not resist the will of one set on the goat's release. He stopped trying to guess where the animal might fall and threw the blankets into the woods.

☙

In rapid succession, the buckets, whose contents slushed with ice, were delivered up to Olmsted. The man discharged the water against the cliff, splashing the goat's neck. The rock encasing the animal began to splinter.

"Stop!" Olmsted shouted.

Eljay, who was attaching the last bucket to a hook, paused. Through the smoke, he saw legs descending the ladder. "Is it alive?" he asked.

Olmsted reached the ground before answering.

"It's already fallen," he said. "It was too smoky to see where it fell or what it looked like."

Both men started searching the base of the cliff. Eljay searched more frantically. The smoke cleared. Starlight dimly illuminated the forest's edge. Eljay perceived something move in front of him. There, he saw the goat's head and neck attached to a bulky fragment of rock. No body extended past this rock. The animal was digging its nose into the leaves, trying to pull itself forward. But it was either too weak, or the rock was too heavy. Eljay ran up to the animal and gathered its head in his hands. He could see no wounds except for a cavity in its forehead where a horn once stood. Lichen had been torn from one of its eyes. The eye, suffused with blood, ticked over Eljay a few times before rotating and becoming glazed.

"Why did I listen to that man? I should've put those blankets down. I know you better than anyone." These are the things Eljay said into the goat's ear.

Olmsted hovered over Eljay and the goat. The man had a look of wonder and disgust on his face. He seemed to be struggling for words. "Malformed," Olmsted said finally. He walked back to the ladder, climbed up, and looked into the hole in the mountain where the goat had been. By the grey light of dawn, Olmsted saw that no body could have ever existed inside it. The concavity was less than a foot deep.

Eljay had not moved, his mouth pressed to the goat's ear. He did not notice Olmsted return.

"It'll smell soon," the man said, almost softly. "There's nothing to do but burn it."

Eljay shook his head. Olmsted hardly existed for him now.

The man had never heard someone talk to a dead goat like that. He gave a last look at the spot where the goat's neck and the granite merged. It was a mistake, some afterbirth that had taken hold. In his long journeys, he had come across things that were not, perhaps, so different. After retrieving the pulley and gathering his tools, Olmsted set off for his trapping cabin. Neither he nor Eljay had anything to say to each other. There was no reason for them to meet again.

☙

Eljay woke in the afternoon. A bird was perched atop the goat's head, tearing at its hair. He flung his arm at the bird, which flew up to a branch and stayed there, eyeing the scene. He guarded the goat's remains for the rest of the day. The next morning dozens of birds amassed in the trees. They seemed eager for his departure.

He realized that he could not dig a grave at the foot of the mountain. Other animals roamed the vicinity. Wolves or foxes might excavate in the night. He worked up his nerve and took the goat under its stiff jaws. He began dragging it, along with the granite block, across the forest. There was a creek a mile away. It was not until dusk, though, that he reached it. The labor was difficult. He often stopped to weep.

The creek was frozen all the way down to the sand. Three days earlier Eljay had had to cut the ice with a handsaw and melt it over a fire to fill the buckets for Olmsted. The handsaw, which was his own, still lay beside the creek. Before long he had carved out a square large enough to inter the goat.

It took some adjustment to get the goat and its conjoined rock into the grave. With his heart beating fast, he bent the animal's neck to fit a corner in the ice. He saw that the cube he had cut from the creek could not be reinserted. So he melted half of the ice in a pot over a fire.

In the twilight, Eljay poured the tepid water over the goat's head until it was submerged, and the water leveled out with the frozen surface. The water did not take long to freeze. No animal that he knew of could burrow into this creek. The goat was safe until spring. The ice would preserve it.

☙

The snows came but fell less than usual. The winter, however, was relentlessly cold. Many times Eljay almost froze to death. His shack could have been sealed with materials from the forest, but he gave himself up to chance.

Slowly the season passed. One day, Eljay woke sweaty and restless. Sunlight bore down on his shack. He crawled outside. The sky was blue and cloudless to the farthest mountains. The snow in the shade of the trees was melting. Streams of water curved down the slope of the granite. Above him, the sun seemed fixed. He thought of nothing but the pleasure of the light. For some time he stood there until, looking at the meltwater, an image of the goat in the creek came to his mind. His body jerked. He ran for the path that led down the mountain.

Eljay came to a stop, his chest heaving. A strong current passed between the remnants of ice along the banks. He rushed into the water and located the block of granite. Using all his strength, he hauled it into the air and shored it. The worst had happened. The current had done its work. A circle, dense with multicolored tissue, marked where the goat's neck once joined with the rock. The force of the water had torn it away. For days Eljay searched the creek. Miles downstream, he waded out of the rapids and returned hopeless to the mountain.

☙

What was there to be gained? Where was he to go? The mountain had become merely an upthrust of dirt and stone. Such a creature as the goat, akin to nothing, could never be found again.

In the heat of summer, Eljay revisited memories until his face looked older than before. But as the leaves changed color, it became clear that his supply of food would not last much longer. There was no choice but for him to depart.

The urgency of his situation turned his mind to the present. He dismantled the shack and the wooden cart the townspeople had given him. It looked as if he had never lived on the mountain. He gathered a few things in a pack and left the cliff behind him.

A month later Eljay walked under the falling leaves. He was far to the north of the mountain. He doubted even Olmsted had ventured into this region.

In a pond he caught a speckled trout. He found a hillside overgrown with wild leeks. Though it tasted bitter, he ate the bark from trees. He moved on with no destination in mind.

A herd of deer appeared from the east and changed direction, keeping pace with him. It was during the rut. Bucks rubbed their antlers against trees. Does squatted and lifted their tails to urinate. Eljay, by some intuition, drifted into their procession. They surrounded him on every side.

For the first time in years, his thoughts flowed without obstruction. The past, he realized, was only a frame of mind. He imagined Olmsted, and all the townspeople who had wronged him, gathered on the banks of a distant river. Tears filled their eyes as the goat's decayed head rose from the water. Its mouth opened as if to speak to them. Its jawbone caught the sunlight. Eljay could not resist laughing.

The Gully Dwellers

I

Things hadn't been going well for me. I thought my life would've worked out a lot better. I was having trouble finding a job. My girlfriend was tired of hearing me complain; she loved me and wouldn't leave me but needed some space. At least a week, she said. No contact. Don't call unless it's an emergency. It'll be good for both of us. I understood. But I came to the wrong place. The worst place.

I drove up to the North Georgia mountains until I had no cell service, ended up in the middle of nowhere, and took a random turn onto a forest service road. After a few minutes the houses and farms petered out and there were just trees. *Might as well get lost*, I thought. So I drove and drove. The road seemed endless; I swear it was a maze. I went up an entire mountain and dipped down it and swerved around and branched off to God knows where and wound up here: the place I can't escape. At first, I thought I'd come to an outdoor Appalachian folk museum. There were all these nineteenth-century log cabins that seemed uninhabited but looked well-preserved.

I was intrigued, so I pulled off beside a creek. It was quite the beauty spot. After checking out the old-timey cabins and walking around the fields I decided that I'd just camp there. No one was around. It was a weird place but a good fit for my mood.

I set up my tent by the creek and ate a snack, but it was still too early to turn in for the night, so I went back over to the cabins and walked across the field into the woods behind them. The trees, mostly pines, were thicker and taller than any trees I'd ever seen before. I was struck by the silence. In fact, I heard no birdsong anywhere, and that's a pretty strange thing for the middle of summer.

I was about to turn back when I saw a flickering light a ways off in the darkness; even at six in the evening, the woods were almost pitch black. I tried to figure out what the light was without going any farther into the forest. But I couldn't make it out.

If someone else was camping, I'd feel uncomfortable. I was in the middle of nowhere; who knows what kind of people camped in this area? Maybe people hiding out. People running from the law. Murderers and rapists.

Yet like a fool I had to see what that light was. I was bored and feeling a little nihilistic. I had an uneasy feeling but decided to just go a few more yards and then head back.

I waded through the rhododendron. There was a figure moving beside the flickering light. *Some weirdo*, I thought. I crept a little closer. I stooped behind a fallen tree and peeked over.

At first my eyes were mesmerized by the flame but then adjusted. Beside a campfire was a man with a stone in one hand. His other hand was splayed on the ground. His gaze was focused on the distant forest, on some point I couldn't see. Suddenly he brought the stone down on one of his fingers; I could hear the bone snap. There was a dark sheen in his eyes—something wrong, malevolent. His beard was like a dripping mass of oil. He brought the stone down on another finger and broke it as well. I couldn't take it anymore and cried out for him to stop. I had to put an end to this madness. The man merely cocked his head but didn't miss a beat as he smashed his thumb to a pulp, which popped like twigs in a fire. The remaining two digits he treated with similar ferocity.

The man then thrust his hand into the flames, and when he took it out it was no longer mangled. It was dirty yet whole. Once again he splayed his fingers on the ground and lifted the stone to start breaking them. It was as if someone had pressed rewind.

My mind went blank, and I fled. I crashed through the forest and back to the clearing and past the cabins to where my car and tent should have been. But they weren't there. There was no sign of my stuff anywhere. The creek rushed past and that was all. Panic hurtled over me. What nightmare was I in? How could everything have been stolen? Who had done it? How would I get back to civilization? I had no food. The night would be cold. I had driven down that dirt road for an hour at least after the last farm.

I howled with rage. The person who had stolen my stuff should be nearby. I could go confront them. But no—they had taken my car, driven off somewhere. They were miles away by now. It made me sick how helpless I was. Tears stung my eyes, but I tried my best to keep it together. *It'll be okay*, I told myself. *You just have to start walking back. There's plenty of water and that's the main thing. You can survive a long time without food. The dirt road won't be impossible to follow in the dark. If the moon is out the gravel will catch its light.*

So I took a deep breath and headed back the way I came. The man breaking his fingers dogged my thoughts, but if I didn't keep a level head, I'd get off the road and end up lost in those godforsaken woods.

II

I walked until my feet started to blister, yet the little creek never swerved away from me; it stayed on my left side the whole time. When I'd driven into this hollow, the road had only followed the creek for a quarter mile or so. Either I was losing my mind, or maybe I had turned in the wrong direction and was heading deeper into the mountains and farther from civilization.

I started running. After a few miles, the same creek and the same trees bordered the road. The sky darkened, and it wasn't long before I'd be at the mercy of the moonlight. I wish I'd been smart and packed a full backpack like my girlfriend Heather always does, with snacks, maps, blister Band-Aids, and bear spray. I'd never been much afraid of bears, but I didn't want to meet one in the dark without bear spray or a knife. I was hesitant to use my phone's flashlight because I didn't want to run the battery down. I'd climbed a few knolls but had not gotten any service. I prayed for a single bar to no avail.

Then from somewhere came a chopping noise. Somewhere not far off in the trees. A heavy, thudding stroke. *Maybe some forest service people are around*, I thought. *Or some hermit in the woods.* I didn't like the idea of running up on someone with an axe, but I didn't have much choice—I had to investigate. The chopping sound got a little closer, and closer, so I went towards it hoping for the best. I passed through the dark archway of the trees into a space without much light.

Chuck, chuck, I heard, even closer.

I looked up into the foliage, hoping for a piece of sky to help me navigate. I did a double take. There was a pale face in the treetops. My breath caught. The pale face, which I thought might be the moon for a moment but was in fact a human face in the leaves, frowned at me. It was hard to gather details about that face, other than that its bald head was peppered with moles.

"Beware the woodswoman," it said with a foreign, old-fashioned accent. "She's always in pursuit."

Suddenly the pale face in the trees was gone.

"Hello? Who's there?" I called. "What did you mean about the woodswoman?"

No answer, of course.

Though I didn't know it yet, that was my first encounter with the Watcher.

In the gloom, a tree tottered.

A heavy thud and click. *Chuck, chuck, chuck.* The sound was only a few trees away.

A giant of a woman loomed up in the half-light. The swinging axe head was as large as a guillotine blade. Her muscles bulged from her tattered overalls. She didn't look me directly in the eyes, but I could tell that she was aware of me. Highly aware. She opened her mouth wide, as in a silent cry of joy or despair.

The woodswoman unwedged the axe from a massive pine, took a great leap, and swung it at a tree closer to me. In her cruel, vacant, unearthly eyes, I saw that she was after me, that she was chopping all the trees between me and her, one by one, until she got to me, her final trunk. She intended to hack away my ribcage, cut me so deep that my upper body would totter and split apart.

Woodchips sprayed my face. The woodswoman crouched down, gathered her energy, and pounced a yard nearer, her head shattering tree branches in her flight.

She raised her axe again and I ran. Behind me I heard a gulp and chop, and the leaf litter crackling under the friction of another great leap towards me.

I looked back and the woodswoman opened her mouth again, stretching it as wide as it would go. When she shut her mouth abruptly, angrily, her lips leaked a dark fluid.

I'm in a nightmare, I thought, *or something like it. I'm trapped in some magician's dark stone.*

Eventually I found the road, twisting like a grey river in the moonlight.

Not far away, coming ever nearer, sounded the *chuck-chuck* of her axe.

I sprinted up the dirt road, back toward the cluster of cabins, realizing what I must do: find the pale face in the trees that had spoken to me. The man crushing his fingers, this woodswoman with her great axe, neither of them had said anything. But the face in the trees, as frightening as it was, had warned me. It was an intelligent creature—an enemy, perhaps, but at least one that could communicate.

"Beware," it had said. "The woodswoman's always in pursuit."

There appeared to be no clear north, south, east, or west in whatever dimension I'd entered, and distances seemed to expand and contract, but as long as I was running away from the axe noises, I had a little hope.

III

I hadn't heard an axe blow for many hours. I had clearly left the woodswoman behind. No pale face materialized in the trees other than the moon. At last, dead tired and hungry, I stumbled back upon the little colony of nineteenth-century cabins. I searched the area again for my car or any supplies that had been dropped, but it was as though I'd never driven there in the first place. I felt like my mind was a high cliff, and I was wandering blindly near its edge.

In the woods I could vaguely see firelight. I wouldn't go towards that self-maiming man again. I listened carefully for the sound of an axe but heard nothing. I was safe for the time being. By some weird logic, it seemed that the woodswoman couldn't chase me freely but had to strike a heavy blow to each tree between me and her before she could hack me down. It would take her a while to catch up. Nonetheless, as the face in the trees had said, she was always in pursuit. I was now her prey.

I had to get some answers. I had to figure out how to escape. Very cautiously, I started investigating the cabins, lit by moonlight. My phone's battery was at fifty percent, so I turned it off. I'd only use the flashlight if I had no choice (my girlfriend would have thought to pack a portable charger).

I called a greeting in each one-room cabin but met only darkness and the smell of ancient wood. Each one had a stone chimney, leaning and crumbling. None of the cabins seemed occupied. Yet there was no dust, no extreme filth in them. They were taken care of by someone. I wished, as in a fairy tale cottage, some spirit had left behind a cauldron of hot stew. Yet this place seemed to hold only a sterile emptiness.

I ventured back into the woods but away from the fire where the man was breaking his bones. I'd never known such simmering fear, never lessening, always about to spill over.

In a clearing in the forest was another old-timey cabin, yet this one, if my eyes weren't mistaking me, sat atop a huge concrete block. It was the most modern thing I'd seen in the area, like a small art museum in a perfect cube, though the cabin on top of it looked as ancient—if not more ancient—than the rest.

I approached the structure and found that the concrete block rose about twice my height and was smooth and sheer, so I couldn't jump up, grab hold of the top, and haul myself over to get to the cabin. It was an anomaly.

I called out but got no answer. Furious, I kicked a rock spotlighted by the moon. I stubbed my big toe and cursed. Though the rock had barely moved, a whispering came from it that I assumed was the patter of loose dirt. I plopped down, my head in my hands. The rock shifted again. I supposed I'd just dislodged it from its pocket in the soil and it was settling into a new position. I heard more whispering beneath it.

"Down here," a voice said.

Run, I told myself, but my body didn't obey. My reason, somehow, was stronger, and reminded me that I'd been searching for the face that could speak. And here, no matter how horrifying, something spoke under the rock.

Hardly breathing, I pushed the rock, which tumbled over. The pale face occupied the hole where the rock had been. It was at once very old, spider-webbed with wrinkles, yet very young, angelic, and childlike.

"Who are you?" I said through chattering teeth. "I need to leave. Can you help me get out of here?"

"Some of the chimneys are safe," the face said with that same foreign accent. It frowned dramatically. Wrinkles like Roman numerals formed on its chin, then became smooth as cream when its expression relaxed.

"How'd you get under that rock?"

"Secret," it said.

"Who are you? Can you help me?"

"The Watcher."

"The Watcher?"

"Call me what pleases you. The Watcher. Cornbee Piper. Sir Vesper, the Jester. Windeve. Hamlin."

"Can you help me?" I repeated.

"I could," it said. "Try the chimneys—the houseless ones that stand alone. No promises, though. But listen here. When you're hungry, whistle this tune, and I'll come with my bag of meat."

The face whistled a snatch of tune I hadn't heard before. Then it sank back into the dirt and the hole was suddenly empty. Hesitantly I touched the dirt at the bottom of the hole, half-afraid a hand would grab me and pull me underground. But the ground was firm, and I could find no outlet beneath it. How had the face appeared there? Could it vanish and reappear anywhere it wanted? What kind of sorcery was this? I hadn't thought occult forces existed. I had always argued with my girlfriend about it. I had a closed mind, she'd said, and only saw half the world. If she was right, and our reality folded into other realities, and there were multiple crossroads and secret doors to other realms, it was too terrible and mind-bending. My brain felt bruised, the wires crossed. I wanted to go back to the way things were, back to Heather.

I heard the distant *chuck-chuck* of the woodswoman coming ever nearer. I had to keep moving. My stomach growled, but I didn't want to whistle the Watcher's eerie tune. I couldn't imagine being so hungry that I'd want that creature to return with his so-called bag of meat. The thought made me sick.

In a daze, I walked onward as the moon set, not knowing where I was headed. In the fading light, little towers rose. They were chimneys, I realized, not connected to any house. Or, rather, the houses once attached to them had disintegrated, and these high stone memorials were all that remained.

"Try the chimneys," the Watcher had said. "The houseless ones."

Could I trust that uncanny face? It had warned me about the woodswoman. It had said it 'could' be trusted, which seemed somewhat ambiguous. The Watcher seemed capable of both help and hurt.

Nevertheless, I went up to a chimney and examined it. For some reason, it had no fireplace. As I was scaling it, gripping the round stones and scrambling up the fifteen feet to the top, the moon disappeared behind the mountains. It was pitch black and no stars came out.

I didn't expect to see anything in the chimney, but since I had already climbed it and perched awkwardly at its top, I peered down into the darkness. And my heart almost stopped.

Deep inside the chimney, a hundred feet down at least—so much deeper than the chimney should have gone—bodies crawled back and forth, in and out of dim light. What those bodies were, whether human or other, I couldn't tell. It terrified me, and I decided I'd rather keep running from the woodswoman than descend into that chimney. But out of nowhere someone or something picked me up with incredible strength, as though I was light as a feather, and threw me head-first down the chimney. I had no time to react, hardly enough to be surprised. My heart told me the Watcher had done it. The flue was just wide enough to let me slip down it, my clothes catching momentarily on rocks that kept me from free falling. But down and down I went, getting scratched all over, nosediving straight for the light and the crawling forms at the bottom.

IV

The chimney descended far into the earth. I'd truly entered some nightmarish wonderland. The wriggling shadows flashed below me, and eventually I fell onto an old mattress at least a hundred feet below ground. Beside me guttered an oil lamp. I lay on the mattress for a moment, stunned, gazing up the towering flue from which I'd just fallen, amazed I was still alive.

Something scuttled over my hand and I jerked it away. I saw nothing except that the mattress was stained with dark patches, maybe blood, and smelled like roadkill. I rolled off it with a queasy feeling. As I did so, something else scampered over my back and leapt into the darkness.

I didn't want to know what these creatures were. Giant rats, most likely, infected with diseases.

I picked up the oil lamp and held it to the darkness. At first nothing moved. I was in something like an ancient sewer pipe, round and made of bricks. I waited; I heard a rustling. I tried to control my breathing and focused on the dark tunnel ahead, watching for any movement.

Whatever comes at you, I said to myself, *just laugh*. That's what I did in horror movies to cope with fear.

Something materialized. A child, I thought at first, crawling slowly towards me. It lifted its cracked, blindfolded face. "Help me," it rattled, raising its tiny arms.

I froze. It continued crawling towards me. The face was half-human, and the creature didn't have any legs. A naked doll, it turned out. There seemed to be burn marks all over it as if it had been set on a grill at different angles.

"Help me," the doll begged. "Please don't eat our bodies. Don't be like the others."

Suddenly a puppet, broken strings trailing behind it, ran out of the darkness and tripped over the pleading doll. I gasped and backed away onto the disgusting mattress. This puppet, I noticed, had its eyes scratched out, probably with a knife. It kept running, crashed into the wall, spun around, and continued on. It pumped its arms, yet I noticed it had no hands, just splintered stumps. In a flash the puppet vanished, and once again I was left alone with the porcelain doll.

Both these mannequins were mutilated. I remembered that I was supposed to tell myself to laugh, but I couldn't manage it.

"Are you going to kill me?" I stammered. That's all I could imagine happening.

The doll's mouth didn't move, but its voice said, "That's funny. I asked for help. Why would I hurt you?"

I was positive the doll would ask me to carry it out of this dungeon, and I shivered at the idea of touching it, but instead it said, "Help me and my brothers and sisters by doing two things: First, don't eat anything the Watcher gives you, no matter how hungry you are. Second, find the invisible tower and escape through it."

"The invisible tower?" I asked, baffled. "What do you mean? How does that help you?"

"No one has ever escaped the gully. If you find a way out, you'll help us die after centuries of suffering."

"What does all this mean?"

"You heard me before, didn't you? About not eating anything the Watcher offers? If you do..."

A different puppet with nails driven into its body ran past us in a blur. There must have been a hundred nails in it. "The Watcher!" it panted as it dove into the darkness.

Suddenly two pale hands passed through the wall and grabbed the doll I'd been speaking to. The hands pried open its mouth, nearly cracking its face apart, and plucked out the doll's writhing red tongue. The pale hands then bashed its porcelain skull against the bricks. The doll convulsed violently.

I sprinted down the tunnel, slightly bent over to avoid banging my head on the ceiling. In my panic, I'd dropped the oil lamp.

Nearly witless, I crashed into a wall and, after shaking it off, searched the bricks with my hands and found that the tunnel branched in a different direction. I ran a bit farther and crashed into another wall and had to find a new way forward. I was lost, it seemed, in an underground labyrinth.

Another doll or puppet, huffing and snorting as if it had respiratory issues, brushed past me, and I nearly jumped out of my skin. For whatever reason, I expected it to stab me with a knife, but it whispered, "Never stop for long." It pattered onwards, its little footsteps fading into silence.

I got down on my hands and knees and crawled as quickly as I could. Every moment I expected pale hands to pass through the walls and rip me to pieces.

Eventually I saw a vague light. I worried about what lay ahead, but I was relieved to have some goal in that dark maze.

I entered a faintly lit chamber. It took my eyes a moment to adjust.

There was another doll, about three feet tall, in a medieval-looking dress with hair of tangled red yarn. The doll's arms and legs were outstretched, and it was stuck to the wall. It gave me the impression of a child being drawn and quartered.

"How do I get out of here?" I asked desperately. I was feeling more frenzied and claustrophobic by the minute. A half hour ago, I would have never imagined asking a doll a question.

The doll's mouth was round as a penny.

It didn't reply. After all, this might be a regular doll, incapable of speech, without consciousness—how dolls should be.

The huffing puppet had told me not to linger long in any one place.

As I picked up the new oil lamp, ready to leave that strange torture chamber, the doll moaned. Its cotton face crinkled, and its button eyes widened.

"Lever in my belly," it groaned. "Pull it and there's a ladder."

"In your belly?" I asked, sick at heart.

"Hurry," it said. "Pull the lever and the ladder will drop."

I put down the lamp and went over to the doll. A chunk of cotton flesh was missing from its stomach. It felt obscene to stick my hand into that wound. *It's just a doll*, I told myself, but I knew that was only half true.

"He's here," the doll gasped. "The Watcher."

That threw my scruples to the wind. I reached into the doll's slick insides, parts of which felt cottony and parts like intestines. Fear kept nausea from overtaking me, and I found a lever, which I pulled. The doll gasped in pain. Its button eyes trembled and then stilled. To the right a ladder slid down and banged against the floor. I mounted it and climbed furiously towards a distant speck of light. I tried not to look down, but at one point I did and could see movement far below in the gloom. Something was after me, most likely the Watcher. The metal rungs of the ladder squeaked beneath me. *Faster, faster*, I told myself, and the speck of light broadened into a patch of sky. My arms and legs were about to give out when I emerged into the outside air.

I'm safe, I thought, and wanted to cry for joy. I don't know why I thought that so soon, just by reaching the earth's surface.

Whatever had followed me touched my shoe lightly, eerily. It inserted what felt like a wooden finger into my sock and scratched my heel. I yanked my foot away and tumbled down from a high chimney into the grass. I waited for the creature to pounce down upon me, but nothing followed me out of that chimney. I blinked at the morning sun and tried to calm the furious beating of my heart.

V

After I fell into the grass, I lay there for a little while, stunned. The chimney I had used as an exit from the underground was also a solitary structure—its house had disintegrated long ago. For a while, I studied its composition, all the details of stone and chinking. But when I heard the ever-nearing *chuck-chuck* of an axe, I stood on wobbly legs and moved off.

I found many more solitary chimneys. Hundreds of them in various states of decomposition. Some, though clearly very old, were almost perfectly preserved; others had withered down to nubs.

I drank from the creek and put some sassafras in my mouth to chew to stave off hunger—a trick my grandmother had taught me. I kept glancing at the trees since I half-expected the Watcher to appear in them at any moment. Before I had sought him, now I fled from him at all costs (the dolls had referred to this creature as 'him', so I took the cue). My heel itched where the strange finger had touched it, and I assumed I was getting a blister. I couldn't deal with investigating my shoe at that moment. I still had all my limbs, and that's what mattered.

In a daze I passed through trees and over boulder-strewn fields. The mountain slopes seemed to retreat every time I approached them. This drove me almost to distraction; climbing a mountain was my best chance at getting cell service, but they always wandered away.

I needed to be searching for an invisible tower but had no idea where to start or if it was just a cruel joke.

Eventually I came to a glen with a squat cabin nestled up against a hill. I approached it cautiously. A woman sat on a rocking chair on the front porch, rocking furiously. I was in her direct line of sight, but she didn't acknowledge me. She wore a white lace bonnet and a dark dress, as though in mourning. Her hands were clasped.

This was another person possessed by some demon. There was no way I'd get closer to her. I'd receive no help from this grandmother. I backed away.

As I did so, another person came into view. It was a nude, hairy man galloping on stilts. He crashed through the underbrush straight for the cabin. I would have laughed if it wasn't for the hunger in the man's expression. The woman in her rocking chair leaned forward, her hands frantic, a wild grief in her eyes. The hairy man took big, long strides on his stilts and thrust out his tongue.

He had increased his speed and was nearly upon the grandmother in her rocking chair when I turned around. This was a horror that would replay throughout eternity, and interfering in it would lead to death—I was sure of that. All these aboveground people seemed to be caught in a dark loop, in a savage dumbshow, that would repeat as long as this place existed.

It wasn't long before the creak of her rocking chair stopped altogether.

I crashed through the woods with tears in my eyes. At some point the blister on my heel started to hurt too badly, so I sat down and took off my shoe. A piece of paper had been inserted into my sock.

I remembered how, as I climbed the ladder, a wooden finger had touched my shoe lightly; it had slid into my sock and scratched my heel. The Watcher or a puppet had inserted a note there.

In hardly legible child's script, it read:

> Long ago he tuk us from home into the mowtain. Manee childran. Others com here lik u by axident. Help us. Hed for Watchers basment. It is in the shape ov a qube. Caben sits on top ov it. Safe plase. Not ov this world. Just run into it and it will opn. Get back strenth for invisibal towr. Old legand says invisibal towr is exit. If u let wudswoman chop u u will see it.

Head to the Watcher's basement to regain my strength and then let the woodswoman chop me up? *Great—what a help*, I thought.

I began to understand that those dolls and puppets were somehow children the Watcher had stolen long ago, that they were half alive, half dead, somewhere between human and mannequin. How did I know that these ancient innocents weren't under the thumb of the Watcher, groomed and manipulated by him into giving me the wrong advice, deadly advice? Had this invisible tower been planted in the dolls' minds to trick me? Who could I trust in this miserable place?

VI

I decided to take the note's advice and make for the Watcher's basement, that out-of-place concrete cube I'd seen before. What choice did I have? I didn't know exactly where it was, but I tried to use a few landmarks to aim for that general direction. At times, this world seemed to be as large as five or six square miles, and at others the size of a big farm.

I walked across a barren field, so massive you'd think a mountain used to be there, but some great force had plucked it away.

Suddenly a figure, like a scarecrow, came straight at me. It danced and kicked its legs. It did little twirls and slapped its legs. It was like a traditional Bavarian dance I'd once seen in Helen, Georgia. Before I could turn and run, the dancing man was beside me as though someone had pressed fast-forward. It was the Watcher. The large, pale, ancient yet child-like face bobbed unnaturally on top of that scarecrow body. Over his shoulder he carried a sack, which he slung down; the contents spilled out.

He frowned at me. "Hungry yet?"

I was terribly hungry, and the items that covered the ground smelled delicious, like fresh pastries. Despite myself, I got down on my knees and picked one up; it resembled a pretzel bite.

I almost popped it in my mouth, but a voice inside me said, "Don't eat anything the Watcher offers."

I examined the warm food in my hands. I scratched some of the breaded crust away, and underneath was a meaty, triangular surface, just like a nose. Its edges, however, were spotted with porcelain. When I broke the crust, the other delicacies were fingers, toes, eyes, and a sizable cut from a stomach with a thimble-like belly button. Here was the mannequins' severed flesh.

"You hesitate," the Watcher said, dancing in place.

"What will happen to me if I eat this?"

"You'll be full. You'll be fulfilled."

I was growing weaker by the moment. I almost fainted. Being that close to food, and not eating it, almost broke me.

"Doesn't it smell nice?" the Watcher continued. "Doesn't it smell jovial?"

"I refuse," I said.

"Then you'll starve and never join the game," he said grimly.

"I just want to go home," I said.

"The entryways to this place are many; you only have to be in a particular state of mind. You desired to get lost, you wanted to disappear, so here you came. Easy as pie. But to escape...that's another matter. That's serious business."

"Just tell me how to leave," I pleaded.

"What's the worst thought you've ever had?" the Watcher asked. "Think of the darkest, most warped fantasy or nightmare, the most harrowing thing you've ever heard or imagined. Your most taboo desire. Some people run from those thoughts their entire lives, but here in my playground, in the land between the mountains, you can embrace that taboo forever and no longer fear anything. Bliss, in a way. Come, stop fearing, stop desiring, eat a yummy pastry, sliced and baked with much care. Forget the world where people deplete you day by day. Eat a goody and you'll become just like the maimed man, the woodswoman, and the grandmother. Those lost travelers, like yourself, live in a nightmare, yes, but they exist in climax. Imagine falling through a thundercloud for eternity, ever struck by lightning yet undying. What a thrill!"

It was like a film had been sped up, and in the blink of an eye the Watcher's sour fingers were in my mouth, prying my teeth open.

I kicked him in the crotch—which felt like nothing more than a bag of straw—and sprinted towards the woods. His pale face appeared in the treetops whenever I looked up. I tried to speed up but couldn't go any faster. I was on the verge of collapse. I couldn't escape him.

Then the concrete block, atop which sat the Watcher's cabin, came into view beyond the trees.

I no longer doubted; I didn't have enough energy to doubt. The note had told me to run into the concrete wall and it would open. I could see no doors. At worst, it was a trick, and I'd knock myself out when I made contact with it. The Watcher's face skipped along the treetops, its body nowhere to be found. *No*, I thought. *I'll risk it all rather than have that demented thing capture me.* I bent my head like a charging rugby player. Either I'd pass through the wall like the note had said, or I'd crack my skull in the process, and that was infinitely preferable to eating the Watcher's pastries and being a prisoner in his playground forever.

I dove head-first into the concrete wall and just like those portals in fantasy stories, I passed through and entered the basement. For a long time, trembling, I waited for the Watcher to follow, but he never did. I recovered a bit, and using my cell phone's flashlight, searched the room for something that could help me. It was dusty and filled with boxes of children's books, VHS tapes from the 80s and 90s, broken furniture, and old, useless backpacking gear. It wasn't a place that I feared. I suspected that the Watcher couldn't access this glitch in his world.

According to the mannequin in the underground, I would glimpse the invisible tower after the woodswoman sank her axe into my side. That made the tower sound like the afterlife, like some turret of heaven's castle. But I was desperate. While I had some wits left, I'd have to trust in improbable methods and unlikely outcomes. Maybe from the top of the tower I could get cell phone service.

I rooted out some duct tape and made a thick vest of old paperbacks—*Goosebumps*, *Boxcar Children*, *Young Indiana Jones*. A poor man's coat of mail. It wouldn't stop the woodswoman's axe blow, but maybe the books would keep her blade from biting so deep. Maybe I'd survive with no more than a shallow nick and have enough strength to find the tower, climb it, and somehow escape. If I found the exit, I'd supposedly destroy this hellscape forever.

For many hours I sat there, afraid to leave and confront the woodswoman. I thought of Heather, and I longed for her. I remembered our giddiness at rock and mineral shows, the countless times we died laughing at fecal humor, the travels out west, the passionate lovemaking. The fights and silences that always resolved themselves, even if we had to take some time apart. The almost uncanny connection we had. We always worked through problems and gave each other space.

I was wrong to have been such a sad sack, so petulant and negative. Even if money was tight, and I wasn't where I wanted to be in my career, I had a lot to be thankful for. I wished I could tell her I was sorry.

Eventually, however, I became too weak to reflect and reminisce. I had to leave or I'd become another relic in that concrete cube.

VII

I ran full speed out of the basement and passed through the wall like a ghost. I expected the Watcher to ambush me as soon as I left my hideout, but I saw no sign of him.

Soon I heard the *chuck-chuck* of the woodswoman's axe. I clenched my teeth and ran towards the sound.

My vest of duct-taped books nearly slipped off multiple times. I should have taped it better. I had no practical skills, however, and had never been good at making things. It would have to do.

What if this is all a trick? I thought again. *A way to get me to commit suicide or maim me so that the Watcher can have his way with me? But why would the Watcher warn me away from the woodswoman in the first place?*

I couldn't parse his logic, if there was any. It all felt scrambled. No matter what, though, I didn't want to die alone in a basement. Better to take a chance, even if the odds were small.

Then I came upon the woodswoman, seven feet tall in her tattered overalls, swinging her axe with muscular arms and leaping for the next tree. She didn't look at me, but I knew she sensed me because her nose twitched.

Chuck.

Three trees away.

Chuck.

Two trees away.

Chuck.

One tree away.

I took a deep breath and tried to focus on a happy memory, on my best times with Heather, on my favorite hike in North Carolina, but couldn't quite conjure any happy feelings. I tried to think of each of my beloved cats, but their faces kept running together.

In slow motion the woodswoman leapt with her axe slung behind her. Gradually the blade arced towards me. Her eyes sparked with joy and met mine for the first time. I was hypnotized by their darkness. The axe sliced through my vest of paperbacks, which obstructed the blow just a little. They kept the blade from cutting the extra inch that would have killed me almost instantly.

I felt a warm gush, searing pain, and a kind of puckering and popping, as if soap bubbles were bursting inside of me. The woodswoman, her axe dripping with blood, stood tall. Her eyes went blank. Wind rocked her, but she didn't shift her feet. Her axe hung at an angle like a branch. She had become as still as the trees around her.

I crawled away. My vision blurred. I managed to unfasten my armor of books. The pain in my side was pulsing, electric, astonishing. Yet I felt as if I were on the scent of some secret trail.

Soon I collapsed onto the dirt road and saw the creek beside which I'd planned to set up camp. It foamed over rapids. I stared at the creek for a moment. Something about it captivated me.

I blacked out for a little while. I awoke and again the creek captivated me. The pain ebbed and flowed. I crawled down to the water and followed it for twenty long yards that felt like a mile. A thick streak of blood followed me. I didn't have long. When my body was about to give out, I came to a waterfall.

An invisible structure sat atop that waterfall. Don't ask me how I knew. Nothing indicated the structure's presence. I blinked, tried to get my vision to stop fading. And suddenly the invisibility cloak, or whatever it was, rippled away, and a dark brown stone tower with a single window rose from the waterfall. It was straight out of a medieval town with high battlements. A stone bridge also appeared before me, leading up to an open door. The tower blinked in and out of sight like a bad lightbulb, but it was always there, visible or not. I dragged myself along the bridge through the door.

Inside the tower, a staircase spiraled out of sight. There was no way I could climb it. I crawled over to it and collapsed. But then, it was as if the tower was turned on end, like an hourglass. For a moment I swear I hovered in the air. Then stairs spiraled below me rather than above. It was as though, by magic, I was suddenly at the tower's top rather than its bottom.

My mind, I thought, *has finally broken*. But I was no longer scared. I almost looked forward to my thoughts leaking away, my body emptying of blood. I didn't mind dying in a medieval tower over a waterfall.

Far away, the water hissed and crashed beautifully. I closed my eyes. When I opened them, the Watcher floated above me. He smiled at me for the first time; he wore dentures of horse teeth.

I tried to say, "Let me die alone," but no words came out.

The Watcher's head lowered, and he kissed me on the mouth, leaving behind a taste that was revolting yet hard to pin down. I had never eaten rat before, but that was what I likened it to.

In a jump cut he no longer hovered a few inches above my face, but sat at my side, kneading something into my wound.

"Stop," I mouthed. It hurt yet felt pleasurable at the same time.

I turned. The contents of his sack were emptied out. He was pressing the pastries, the mutilated limbs of the doll and puppet children, into my wounded side. I was naked. I couldn't resist him.

"My son, my son," the Watcher hummed. "We can't let you die. Otherwise it'd just be me, now that you've overturned the tower. I was happy to be king of the land between the mountains, but I'm also happy to go back to the world I came from with no one but you. The children I stole have passed on. The lost travelers have passed on, too. You won the game and helped them all. You freed them. What a saint! Now you'll be my son, my only son. I always viewed those thankless children as nieces and nephews. The lost travelers were like loyal friends. But now! I've always wanted a child. Flesh of my flesh, tongue of my tongue. We'll have so much fun together."

He spat on my wound and continued to knead in the body parts of the mannequins. It felt as if wet clay were numbing the pain. New blood seemed to pump into my system.

A ray of sunlight shot through the tower's only window. The Watcher took out a full-length mirror from somewhere and redirected the light onto my side, where he'd been kneading. The light heated up my body immediately, as though my torso was in an oven.

"Time for you to bake in the sun. It'll be an hour until you're done. I have some things to wrap up, some skin to swallow. Don't want to leave any trace. You just lie here and let your wound leaven."

"I'll kill you," I said, finally strong enough to speak.

"Don't talk to Papa that way!" he said. "I'll be back soon. Then we'll roll you down the stairs, and *voila*! We'll be back home, in the old town by the big river. You'll love it there. Now be a good son and bake in the sunlight. Don't move a muscle. What an adorable, bearded boy you are!"

In a flash the Watcher was gone. I couldn't escape down the stairs—that led to the old town, as he called it. Yet the window was a mere slit, too narrow to jump out. I was trapped.

Moving an arm was all I could manage. I turned on my phone. My battery was at one percent, yet I had one bar of service. I couldn't believe my eyes. I called Heather. The phone rang once. It rang twice. I pleaded for my luck to change, just this one final time. It rang a fourth time and a fifth, and I got her voicemail. It could have been worse. I told her that I loved her, that I loved my family, and that I was trapped somewhere in the vicinity of Fiddle Gap. "Help," I said. "Try to get lost and then you can find me, as crazy as that sounds. I'll be on the other side of the invisible tower above the waterfall. In the old town by the big river. I'm a prisoner of the Watcher." Then my phone died. And that was that. Maybe the police would be able to locate its final ping.

Now the wind blows and the tower trembles. The Watcher is on the way to claim his prize. I have an ace up my sleeve, however. Heather is resourceful and twice as smart as me. If the police can't find me, she just might. And while she sometimes gets tired of me, she loves me and would never abandon me. She will search for me until hell freezes over—in this world or another. If I'm caught in some dark loop, some nightmare engineered by the Watcher, she'll find a way to break the curse. She will be the hero of this story. I'm merely the catalyst, the reason to leave.

II

DARK AGES

Unfug the Hermit

Unfug the hermit was very cold. The king had forbidden him to cut the trees around his hermitage for firewood. He used too many branches, the king had said, and the forest was dwindling; if Unfug was caught stealing more wood—and the royal forester knew every twig in the forest—he'd end up as fuel for the king's own furnace, and his body would cook porridge for a day.

It was deep winter, and icicles hung from the hermit's dirty thatch eaves. He thought of Saint Sebaldus of Nuremberg, who had saved a peasant couple from freezing to death by lighting a fire with icicles. Unfug chafed his blue fingers and bit on them to revive the blood. Why couldn't he, like Saint Sebaldus, call on the power of God to coax a spark from a pair of icicles?

He lit a candle stub, shuffled into the frosty night, and broke two icicles from the eaves. Back inside, he closed his eyes and licked the grime from his lips. He prayed to God to favor him like Saint Sebaldus and ease his suffering.

Unfug rubbed the icicles together, sawing off chips, cold water from the friction making his hands even more miserable. No flame erupted. He cried Jehovah's name and tossed the icicles into the fireplace. They shattered like cheap stained glass and his cottage became even more dark and desolate than before.

God thought less of him than Saint Sebaldus, which was no surprise. He took out his half-decayed wooden effigy of Christ on the cross and kissed it. Unlike some hermits, he'd never performed any miracles or experienced a mystical vision. The only notable event from his three years as a hermit was when one Sir Gawain, in quest of a Green Chapel, had stopped by his cottage to ask for directions. Otherwise, Unfug had fasted and prayed and meditated on eternity when he wasn't being harassed by the king, his knights, and the forester.

What if he prayed to the devil, just once, for relief from the cold? Maybe the devil would value him more than God. And he could always confess and repent. God would forgive him one minor indiscretion.

He went out to break off two more icicles. With the devil's name in his heart, he touched the icicles together, ever so delicately. They immediately burst into flame, and he threw them into the hearth, where they lit the tinder and started a merry blaze. His skin heated, then his bones, and even his stomach warmed as if filled with freshly baked bread.

Unfug was ecstatic. He had never felt such joy when debasing his flesh and worshipping God. He broke more icicles and threw them into the roaring fire. He amassed all the icicles from the eaves and soon the fire belched smoke and threatened to spill out into the room.

Then, in a corner, Unfug saw a dark, spiraling walking stick, about the size of one a child would carry. It was attached to something at its base. A little shadow-man, it turned out, very tiny indeed, like a burnt gingerbread man. It had no face, and from it projected a twisting horn five times the size of its body. It just crouched there, a nub of darkness, dancing in and out of the firelight.

The tiny shadow man seemed to tacitly approve of the hermit's actions—to even urge him on.

Unfug's flesh positively sizzled. He was now, for the first time in years, a living man rather than a near-corpse. His blood circulated with such rich beats that his mouth tasted sweet. The flames jumped out and consumed his few possessions—his jug, bedroll, cooking utensils, Christ effigy, Bible stand, and the Bible itself. He laughed. He wouldn't miss them.

Peasants from the nearby village gathered around the burning hermitage. Unfug joined the spectators outside and snapped more icicles from the branches and tossed them into the bonfire that was once his cottage. Amazed, one woman followed his lead, and when her icicle entered the pyre, a fireball gushed from it. A child imitated her. Soon all the peasants threw their spears of ice. They called the hermit a wonderworker, a saint. They all reveled in the joyous heat, which had been denied them as well—in fact, quite a few men had had hands chopped off for illegally felling and poaching. The king had forced everyone to use low-grade coal and peat.

As the rotten beams of his hermitage collapsed, Unfug could still glimpse, in a patch of darkness, the little shadow man with the spiraling horn.

The peasants rolled up carts full of icicles taken from their own homes and added them to the conflagration.

The king with his glinting crown, followed by his retinue of knights and the sullen forester, arrived at the scene. The trees were now lit like candles. The entire forest was burning. Timber ruptured, blackened, and bubbled. The branches withered to wavering lines of black yarn and the deep snow melted and evaporated. The king shouted commands that no one heeded; even the forester was mesmerized by the flames licking the starlight. No one knew how to save the king's forest, and the royal newcomers couldn't quite understand why the peasants kept dumping icicles into the inferno; some assumed it was a sad attempt to extinguish the fire.

The circle of people around the hermitage widened and widened as the wildfire spread.

The forest had been beautiful. A wonder of evergreens and vibrant moss and birdsongs. It was also a great source of income for the king, a protected space that would help expand his castle complex; if any lumber was left over from building his towers, it would provide raw material for a new cathedral bearing the name of Saint Walpurga, enemy of witches and the whooping cough.

Suddenly, through the fiery trees, an angel galloped in the form of a white steed with a flowing silver mane. The horse glittered like snow in the sunlight.

Unfug's ecstasy died when he saw the white steed. He came back to his senses. He felt raw inside. Here was God's punishment. He waited for the steed to trample him to death; he waited for the earth to crack open and for a swift descent to hell. What circle of damnation would he enter?

The horse's eyes were like drops of honey in dishes of milk. There was a little cavity in its forehead, as if a jewel had once fit there, some heavenly sapphire.

The steed galloped straight into the mound of embers where Unfug's cottage used to be. And this vision Unfug would never forget in his long life. The little shadow man leaped from the flames, and the steed lowered its white forehead to welcome it. The tiny demon landed in the cavity in the creature's forehead and curled himself into a tight ball—

the fit was perfect—so that only his dark, twisting horn emerged from between the unicorn's eyes.

For it was a unicorn now, a tangle of demon and angel, heaven and hell. The king, his retinue, and the peasants gawked in wonderment, not even shielding their eyes from the bright, painful flames. The virginal beast, with the little horned demon riding its forehead, galloped up into the sky. The trees of the forest stretched and broke their roots and followed the unicorn into the celestial spheres like a thousand burning arrows.

Left behind was a hill of icicles, un-melting, otherworldly. Unfug crawled towards it across the broken dirt, which was icy with no vestige of heat. The unicorn and the burning trees were as far off as a galaxy now. Unfug felt a new kind of cold that didn't hurt but sharpened his senses and thoughts. An invigorating, passionate cold. The crowd—including the king and forester—clasped their hands in prayer as the hermit parted the icicles and entered the frozen hill, his new home, a fit habitation for a holy man who had seen his last miracle.

Confessions of a Gnome

It wouldn't be a lie to call me a kind of demon.

I can secret myself in rays of light. When alchemists gaze in their show stones, I fly into those warped, mineral worlds and perplex the knowledge seeker. Nowadays, fewer and fewer humans look into crystals, hoping to speak with an elemental spirit, but those who do devote much energy to it.

Inside their stones I casually braid my beard, chew on bars of metal, or pass through a series of doors. The observers rave. What mysteries am I communicating? What do my actions symbolize?

There are landscapes inside crystals. Interiors with distant vanishing points. If I could, dear listener, I'd take you inside one. Together we'd weave around primeval spars, pass through speckled clouds, and shrink and expand and triple ourselves in the bending light.

The insides of stones are chilly, but pleasantly so.

I'm a solitary type. As far as I know, I'm one of only a few gnomes. I don't like to share mineral spaces with others. There's a legend that some gnomes have been trapped in lightless places by warlocks—a story I doubt, because there's always some ray troubling the darkness, candlelight or starlight or a vague glitter that humans can't see with their weak, gradually decaying eyes.

There are only a couple of beings I'm on familiar terms with. The devil is one of them. I rather like him.

Every century or so, he cries, "Fly hither, gnome friend. Gee up."

The devil wanders the mountains and valleys at night. He takes the shape of a child and carries a walking stick. His eyes are dark, blind marbles, but his face is pale and cratered with acne scars. If you glance at his face and then at the moon, sometimes you get confused. Though he expresses himself with a child's eagerness and innocence, he's very, very old—much older than me.

I flash across a latticework of moonbeams and materialize in a crystal inclusion on a mountain face. The devil peers at me with his blank eyes as if he can see perfectly fine. He taps the crystal with his walking stick.

"It's been ages since we played a game," he says.

"What do you have in mind?"

"You pretend to be me, and I'll pretend to be you. We'll switch roles."

I'm not afraid of the devil, but I'm wary, despite my natural esteem for him. I don't give him an answer immediately. I take my time pondering the question to remind him I'm not subject to his will.

I also chart out lines of escape, just in case. The devil has never tricked me, but that could change.

"Tell me the rules of the game," I say.

"The rules are simple," the devil says. "Become me for a while, and I'll become you."

"You go first," I respond.

His idea pleases me. I try not to show him how excited I am. It's difficult to hide my smile.

The devil scratches a pit of inflamed skin. He scratches another and another and soon his face sprouts a beard, reddish in the moonlight. It's hard to tell whether the hair is genuine hair or thickened blood. He puts on his head a curved hat that resembles a horn. He throws his walking stick into the air. In a flash it turns into a crystal bubble that engulfs him. Inside the bubble, he braids his beard with a grave, meditative expression. He opens a door in a sheep's stomach and walks through it into a firelit scene. He squeezes juices out of minerals.

I'm mesmerized. I applaud. What an impression! I even catch myself trying to make meaning out of his stunts, like all the poor alchemists and their lackeys who wrinkle their brows, desperate to interpret my actions in their show stones. They always exclaim nonsense like: *Hark! An angel of the astral plane! The symbols cannot be evil—they are an incorruptible quintessence. This gnome provides a bridge between the terrestrial and celestial. It's a messenger of God!*

In my fit of glee, I don't see the devil turn back into a child holding a walking stick. But there he is.

"Your turn," he says.

His cloak flutters in the wind.

I angle myself so that the light splinters me. I reassemble into an acne-scarred child brandishing a fiery walking stick. I find a zigzagging fracture in the crystal and stalk along it as if it's a mountain peak. When I encounter a dark particle, I treat it like a lost soul and make a deal with it.

It's a poor performance compared to the devil's. My joy fades, and I'm ashamed. I realize how little I know about him—whereas he knows a great deal about my business. Why does this surprise me? He's older and more powerful. His domain is larger than light and mineral.

Nonetheless, like a good sport, the devil applauds. It even seems genuine, and I remember why I like him.

"Well, what do we do now?" I ask.

"Tell me the secrets of the earth," he whispers.

We both laugh.

"No, seriously," I say.

"Give me some advice," he says. "I recently learned there's another devil on the moon—my twin. The angel, King Hagonel, confessed this to me before I decapitated him, and upon further investigation, it doesn't appear he lied." He puts his walking stick up to his eye like a telescope. "I believe I can see the imposter now, traipsing about on white mountains as if he walks on long spoons."

"And you'd like me to help you get to the bottom of this rumor."

I don't hide the disappointment in my voice; I dislike when others have ulterior motives.

"You don't have to," the devil responds politely. "Truly. Our game was fun. I won't begrudge you if you leave."

I'm encouraged by his tone. Plus, having just done my best to imitate him, I'm slightly annoyed at the idea of someone else doing it—some more convincing imposter—even if it's in another sphere.

"Your problem," I offer, "is that you can ride the wind, but not light. You cannot reach the moon."

"Precisely," the devil says. "Though I'd love nothing more. I'm fascinated by the moon."

"It is beautiful."

"My lot is an enviable one, I confess; but if I could live on the moon, I would. What a quiet life!"

I'm not sure how to respond.

"If you do this for me," the devil continues, "I'll grant you eternal life!"

Once again we laugh.

For a moment I reflect. I haven't performed a favor for someone in millennia. It's not exactly in my nature. I fly from crystal to crystal, bathed in light, eating hot atoms like apples. I experiment. I perform in dumbshow. I hibernate and teleport and explore the infinity of minerals across the earth, which have a music of their own—eerie, chiming bells that I never grow tired of.

My life is very rich.

But the devil makes me laugh. He revives something lost in me and breaks the fast of my solitude. He makes me desire something new.

I wonder how the moon has changed after all this time.

I wink at him.

"I'll be back in a flash…or two."

As I chart my trajectory, I grow nervous (a sensation I haven't felt since I don't know when). The extra second it will take to reach the moon, speeding through that airless medium, is something I haven't experienced in a long time. It isn't dangerous, however. I realize that I've grown far too used to the patterns of my life here on this planet. I should get out of my element more.

The devil is doing me a favor, after all.

In a blip, first windy then hollow, I enter a faceted crystal on the moon.

It's different there than I remember. The moon used to be covered in snow. Nothing but glittering ice crystals as far as the eye could see—which I could inhabit, of course. Now there's white stone. There's a complex geography, too: humps and brows and swirling cavities of rock.

Over the horizon comes a little boy. It does appear, like the devil said, that his double walks on spoons, a foot in length, perhaps; his shins merge into the handles and the bowls act as shoes. The boy has a jumpy, unbalanced, yet speedy gait. As he approaches, I see that his face is almost an exact replica of the devil's. Yet his acne is active rather than passive, convex instead of concave. The earth's mountain ranges seem to be woven across his face in the form of pimples.

He carries no walking stick. His expression is calm and content.

He springs over to a rock feature that resembles a nose. With one of his spoon feet, he scoops out some dust from the nostril. Then he shuffles over to a stone that looks like a giant's eyeball. Once again, with a spoon foot, he scrapes some detritus from the eyeball's rim. Another formation is a ten-foot-tall ear; the false devil goes over to it and worms his head into the canal as if to relay a message.

My sight adjusts. This entire landscape is composed of fragments of faces, like the fossils of giant men.

There's a cracked stone foot with fat toes. That smooth, round hill over there could be a shoulder or a rump. The surface I occupy is flattish, oblong, and white like a dusty tongue.

Are these the false devil's sculptures? Or a race of long-petrified moon people?

I've seen about all I want to see. I seek out a ray of light to ride back home.

Just then an eyeball—a living eyeball—presses against my crystal.

It's the false devil.

"Who are you?" he asks. His voice is exactly like my friend's.

I don't feel like parlaying with an entity I know nothing about. Nor am I in the mood to perform stunts to mystify him.

Suddenly, my crystal shatters, and I break into countless fragments. In a trice, though, I reassemble into a shard, one hundredth the size. The false devil has just attempted to hurt me, I realize; he struck me with one of his spoon feet.

"You're not welcome here, spy," the false devil hisses. "I don't want any earth spirits corrupting my tranquility. I'm a busy caretaker and my children need tending to. Begone!"

His teeth are closing over me. I can't believe it. He intends to swallow me. In the depths of his throat, I glimpse a darkness I've never imagined—a darkness I thought was only the stuff of legend. That stomach of his must be supernaturally lightless. I would never escape it. Not for an eternity.

At the last millisecond, I leap into a thread of light in a gap between his teeth and re-materialize back on earth, by the true devil, where the wind blows and the trees flutter.

With affection, the true devil taps the crystal I've entered with his walking stick.

"Took longer than I expected," he says. "But no matter. Are the rumors true?"

I still haven't quite gathered my wits.

"Which rumors?"

The devil bites his lip. "The ones about the imposter."

"Yes, all too true."

I feel incapable of saying more. I'm haunted by the darkness of the false devil's gullet.

My friend's face falls. "This is sore news."

"Why?" I mutter.

"There's some change afoot. This pretender is even younger than you—have you considered that?"

I haven't. I shake my head.

"What does it mean?" I ask.

The devil doesn't answer. He gazes at the moon, then at the labyrinth of valleys below us.

"Did my twin look happy? Did he seem content with his work?"

"I suppose."

"Does he love the moon?"

"I don't know," I say. "It appears that way."

The devil seems further troubled. I begin to suspect I should have lied about his twin's happiness.

"And did he ask about me? About his older brother?"

"No," I reply. "There wasn't time. He tried to swallow me."

The devil tries to look grave. It doesn't suit him. Despite myself, I start laughing, and he laughs, too.

"He tried to swallow you?"

"Oh yes, into the darkest of stomachs."

"A narrow escape?" he asks.

"Very narrow."

"Well, until next century," he says, bowing to me. "Thank you, old gnome. I won't forget this favor."

I bow in turn. "I won't say *my pleasure*, but it was a memorable adventure."

The devil smiles.

Already he is wandering the summit of a distant mountaintop. And below this mountain the sun is rising.

I wonder, dear listener, if I should have lied to the devil. If I should have told him that the moon was an empty ruin, that the figure he glimpsed was a mirage, an afterimage of his own sovereign self. I fear what would happen to this world if the devil neglected his duties because of envy and longing. Without him, there would be no way to vandalize and re-fertilize beauty. Even the light would miss him.

For the first time in ages, I feel lonely. I wonder if there will come a day when I yearn for another kind of life. When discontent eats away at my soul. Perhaps this will occur when the last alchemist throws away his show stone; there aren't many of those mad occultists left, after all. I suppose I should appreciate them more and give my favorites a shred of wisdom. I must keep watch over earth and sky as well. I don't doubt that, eventually, my nemesis will appear, some version of the devil on the moon, a beast of a gnome that can ride both light and darkness.

Gruelkey

Merlin passed through rows of weathered columns and decapitated statues, his long beard fluttering behind him. Beyond lay a grey-brown moorland. Most of the trees had been hacked down in the last century, and heather, birch, and willow scrub thrashed in the wind. Merlin was a youngish wizard, yet to make his mark, and the challenge ahead would gauge how far he had advanced in the dark arts.

He squelched across the boggy soil, stabbing his staff into it with each stride, until he crested a hill and glimpsed the object of his journey. Within a saucer-shaped bog rose a megalith of granite as high as a tower. It must have been a hundred feet tall. Speckled with feldspar and blooms of lichen, it lanced the mud and moss like a giant's needle. With Merlin's occult vision, he could discern every detail of the stone even from a mile away. He descended the slope towards his quarry.

The hill dwellers of this region called the bog "Trud Mouldy" and the stone "Gruelkey."

The moorland and the great monolith rising from it looked precisely as they had in his prophetic vision. Even the weather, with low-hovering clouds and muffled sunlight, appeared the same. This stone, Gruelkey, would serve as the first tower, the keystone, so to speak, of Camelot, the legendary kingdom to come; it was imbued with ancient magic far older than Merlin. He had to be careful. This was no Celtic monument, no Druidic temple. Here was a relic of a past not even a wizard could comprehend, a remnant of an ancient British sorcery that survived in no books or traditions.

In Merlin's vision, he had summoned all his power and moved Gruelkey a thousand miles to the site of Camelot, at this time nothing but an empty field. The effort would nearly kill him. His prophecies, however, were never wrong, so he put his faith in his knowledge and skill.

The ground grew soggier, and his boots were sucked into the peat. For the first time, he noticed boulders, placed at regular intervals, encircling the bog. It surprised him that he had not seen them before. They implied protection; they were Gruelkey's guardians.

Merlin trudged onward, yet after a long time, Gruelkey still loomed a half mile away. The landscape, every time he nearly attained the stone, seemed to reach a heathery arm across his path, to fold itself and force him into a gully angled in the wrong direction. The landscape heaved without moving.

Here was more evidence of that ancient magic, still potent after millennia. It nearly took his breath away. He couldn't imagine one of his spells lasting beyond a century. It made him feel weak and vulnerable in this forsaken place.

He jerked his beard, and his head wobbled from side to side like a bell. He needed to shock himself back to his senses. The magic of this heath was pulling him away from his true self. He muttered an old nursery rhyme to calm his heart and then turned inward, to the demon spirit that twisted like beautiful green ivy across his soul. With secret words he awakened this spirit and directed it to reveal the pathway to the bog.

The hills hazed over then peeled apart. The magic was unzipped. He stood beside one of the boulders that circled the bog.

Merlin had moved standing stones before. To honor the dead at Salisbury, he had dismantled Stonehenge and transported it from Ireland to Britain. But the stone before him leaped into the sky and was seven or eight times the size of Stonehenge's most massive trilithon.

As he passed through the zone of boulders, Gruelkey vibrated, twisted slightly as if to get a better look at him. The clouds seemed to spin around its high summit. He gathered his strength and sent his demon out over the megaliths to sedate them, because in some half-conscious way, they were now aware of him and his intentions and sizzled with an electric malcontent. At any moment they might strike.

He muttered another incantation and a dark violet dome spread above the stone and draped the landscape like a royal dress. His spell was powerful and locked the entire site in a cold, listless state. The invisible hands reaching from the boulders trembled arthritically and fell limp.

Merlin regained some of the confidence that had wavered, smiled and picked at a booger, and slogged toward the imposing rock, thigh-deep in bog slush.

It was time. He closed his eyes. He whispered to his staff, then broadcast his demon and molded it into a giant with adamantine hands. Like a puppeteer, he directed the giant's grip to Gruelkey. The stone was in a stranglehold, and he proceeded to uproot it from its anchorage.

Gruelkey hardly budged at first. He had to exert so much energy that he feared his brain would split, but at last there was movement, a slippage, a far-off tearing underground, and the stone dislodged. Merlin guided it up. The foundations had been laid deep, but soon the monolith floated above the bog.

Not quite floated. A thin arm of bog filth clung to the bottom of the stone. The colossal demon that Merlin controlled heaved again, yet only more of this muddy root was exposed, like an umbilical cord.

The root was strangely contoured. Almost statuesque. More: there were faces in the slimy cord. In fact, what clutched the stone was a weave of bog bodies. Men, women, and children, dead and thousands of years old; they were the color of tanned hide, crushed together, holding on to Gruelkey for dear life even in death. Merlin could see the reddish beard stubble on the face of a man half turned to coal. Melting faces without eyes. Open-work bonnets on heads cooked over a fire. Perfectly preserved hands and feet connected to nothing but sacks of skin. Ears that had migrated down necks. Braids of exquisite hair adorning what looked like a rotten, collapsed pumpkin. Mouths open to show rows of teeth, some white and others reduced to seeds.

Merlin was amazed. In his vision there had been no bog bodies chaining Gruelkey to the bog. He had foreseen himself, aided by his demon, hauling off the stone without impediment, its surface clean and grey and glinting with minerals. There had been no umbilical cord. And who had ever heard of a rock pinned down in such a way? What had he missed? What had he neglected? Never before had one of his prophecies been fragmented, partial. And the great work had only just begun. Uther Pendragon had been recently crowned king, and Arthur was not yet conceived. He quaked at what this augured; from his boyhood, he'd studied his visions like complex paintings, memorizing each detail. They had served as the guideposts for his entire life.

He attempted to scythe through the braid of mummies, but they somehow resisted, and the effort nearly caused him to drop Gruelkey. Here again was magic beyond his reckoning. How could flesh—and leaky, buttery, decomposing flesh at that—resist the sharp bite of his spells?

There was nothing for it. He must continue the work of uprooting the monolith. He refocused. He and his giant double strained with the weight and made more progress; Gruelkey rose higher into the air. But with this progress came more bog bodies, an impossibly long rope of corpses. Blindfolded children. Ripples of skin stamped with decayed fabrics. Bodies twisted in torture. One head a collage of potatoes. A torso stretched twelve feet long. A mouth vomiting a dirty rope. An exposed brain, chalk-white and shrunk to the size of a fist. A stomach overflowing with gravel.

Were these people ancient victims of sacrifice—peasants, kings, or wizards like himself? Worshippers of forgotten gods or of the star Endoost, the heaven's mulberry orb, that had suddenly winked out of existence the winter before? Or were they another set of guardians, more potent than the circle of boulders—foes to any wizard crazed enough to extirpate their altar?

Up and up came the cord of bodies, at least fifty feet long. When Merlin was almost on the point of defeat and despair, the final body ripped from the earth. The corpses fluttered from the stone like a tail.

Once again Merlin tried to slice the bodies from the rock. He used every cutting spell he knew. He employed his staff in creative, untried ways. But still the broken root of corpses clung to their stone fruit.

Camelot must have this monolith as its first tower. He had seen it. He had felt it. To disobey a directive given by the dark powers would be like breathing water. He would have to take Gruelkey, which he'd rename the Tower of Evel Vrail, to the plot of Camelot and plant it as it was, root and all. He would have to let the bodies of an ancient, unknown, fearful people coil below the castle like a curse.

As Merlin flew south with the stone and its flapping tail, trembling with the magical effort, he feared for the retreat of his powers and the reign of Arthur, whose image had heretofore bathed his mind with starlight. Already, even before his king was born, he was sowing secrets and riddles that he could not solve, even if commanded to. The chivalric future would be a haunted one. It pained him. He would have to become a different kind of wizard than he had wanted.

Spring, Glacier

Orm Glacier crimped up the volcano for a mile, dirty blue to dazzling white. Sharp moraines and arêtes pierced the ice here and there and smoke curled from the summit caldera. But down in the foothills, purple and pink with arctic thyme amid stones round as trolls' shoulders, all was gentle and peaceful while two old friends, Vikings turned farmers, wandered rather aimlessly in the mild weather, cool wind from the north mixing with warm wind from the south to make a perfect day. Such days, of course, were rarities in Iceland, and the friends used it to their advantage.

Koll was squat and muscular. Though only thirty-five, his beard, which swelled across his torso and reached his waist, was yoghurt-white. He wore an imported linen long-shirt, a cloak pinned with a bronze brooch, and goatskin boots. An iron halberd rested on his shoulder. Ulfar, on the other hand, who was the same age as his friend, boasted a well-sculpted black beard with a distinct point, and was lean and tall and wore an outfit of the commonest wool.

Sheep dotted the upland pastures. A fox disappeared into the moss.

"This is a strange land we've found," Koll said. He shifted his halberd to the other shoulder.

"Yet it's been profitable for you," Ulfar said.

"My farm has grown, yes. There's no more lichen-eating like in the old days, no sucking the insides of shells or eating rotten shark fermented in piss. My family and workmen dine well."

"The gods have favored you."

"I make my sacrifices. As do you."

"And yet look at me," Ulfar said. "You've accomplished so much and I'm worse off than when we came here. Perhaps I should have stayed in Norway." He paused. "My wife divorced me. I know you heard."

"Yes," Koll said. "And I'm sorry to hear it. A bad business and you were treated unfairly. If I had been on this side of the country, I would have intervened on your behalf. I've missed you, old friend."

Koll put a hand on Ulfar's shoulder. The latter beamed at his friend's touch. How many years had it been since they adventured together as boys, plying the iceberg-strewn waves? Always in each other's company, equals in hope, their scents familiar as a mother's. Ulfar could not believe Koll, a powerful chief, would condescend to touch him so familiarly and be so kind, and yet he felt ashamed for being proud that his friend still acknowledged him as worthy of attention.

"It's been a decade since I've seen you, at least," Koll mused.

"At least," Ulfar said, still transported by that sign of friendship which had just slipped from his shoulder.

They walked side by side in silence for a while, vanishing in and out of a hot spring's steam.

"It has been hard for you, then," Koll said at last.

"Not easy."

"How have you lived?"

"After my livestock was confiscated, I collected driftwood and bog ore. Chopped birch. You saw that forest near my home—it's considerable. And once I came across a beached whale. I suppose I haven't been completely luckless."

"Yet you have no men to help you?" Koll asked. "Not even that cousin—I forget his name?"

"None but myself. Day and night I fight a great emptiness. No Celts, no magicians or bears—my fight now is against a sense that life has been a waste, that I've had no passions, no talents, no direction. I can't keep or inspire love. I'm sorry," he said, trailing off. He couldn't believe he'd revealed so much. It was sickening, dizzyingly shameful, and in the face of an old friend transformed by success after success. He was afraid Koll would think he was angling for help.

Instead Koll said, "At least your beard is still black and beautiful. Look at mine. This is my price."

The shorter man tugged his yoghurt-white beard, dripping with steam.

Ulfar smiled. He couldn't help himself. "All is not lost—you are right. I'm still a handsome giant compared to you."

"You're a veritable elf," Koll said. "A worthy concubine to any god."

Their laughter died suddenly.

At first, they took it for a road of undulating rock. But it was something else. Out of the moss and basalt a vast branch, wider than ten merchant ships set bow to stern, writhed out of the ground, hugging the volcano's base and then shooting into the distance for a mile or more before vanishing into the earth again. The two friends approached it, passing hands over its rough bark. It was a tree limb, gigantic and otherworldly. A splinter ran through the pad of Koll's finger. Being a hardy man used to minor injuries, he plucked it away with no sign of pain.

"An offshoot of the world tree?" Ulfar asked.

"Yggdrasil," Koll said, his rough voice full of awe.

"Could Iceland sit on a new branch? A tenth? Is this land we've stumbled upon so wondrous?"

Koll lifted the halberd above his head and, with a mighty down-swing, drove the blade into the wood. Golden fluid bubbled from the cleft.

"This island is as distant from Norway as the moon," Ulfar said. "Is it so surprising that Yggdrasil, its veins running with the mead of the gods, should undergird us? Iceland must be a leaf on its best branch."

Koll ripped up moss to clean his blade, which was sticky as with honey.

"Perhaps it is a sign," Koll said. "A blessing from the gods. You have been down on your luck, old friend. Whereas I have so much land that it would take a long winter's night to carry a torch across it. I believe this gift is meant for you and that the fates have decreed it. Why not drink of the sap of this great tree? It smells delicious. If it be Yggdrasil, I've heard that a draught of its sap bestows wealth and wisdom. If it be a vast, ancient, unmagical tree native to this land that we've newly discovered, then the draught cannot harm you. Either way, I wager you won't regret it."

Koll's counsel didn't seem unreasonable. Boys, hardly thirteen, who had fought an Irish sorcerer in a tower and been wounded by his Christian spells and martyr's recklessness in wielding a sword, could not help but have each other's best interests at heart; however, it was a memory of being encased in frozen spray on the tossing North Sea, embracing Koll for warmth, inhaling his friend's breath as the oars broke ice, the wind howling and men commanding them to return to rowing, that spurred Ulfar to act.

What was the point of being so doubtful, so hesitant all the time? The gash in the wood leaked amber blood, inviting him, making his mouth water. He pressed his lips to it and swallowed the resiny fire.

Koll's face crinkled with joy, and he laughed uproariously as Ulfar coughed.

"Is it that bad?"

Ulfar held up his hand and coughed for another minute until his face reddened. He took a water-skin from his friend and gulped. Koll kept chuckling, whapping him on the back.

"The sap was glorious," Ulfar said finally. "No, I'm not kidding. Better than the mead at Oddgeir's hall. The stuff just got stuck in my throat. And it has a keen bite like liquor. You should try it."

"No, no, let's not divide our blessings. You take the full portion."

"In that case," Ulfar said, "time for another drink."

"That's the spirit! Soon you'll be the king of an entire fjord."

 ☙

The friends climbed a knoll with an even better view of the great, writhing tree branch. From this angle, they could see that a section of the bark was burnt and ashen. They sat side by side, just touching, feeling the shadows of clouds swoop over them. They debated good-naturedly about the branch's length—a mile as the crow flies, but a furlong more if one counted all the twists and turns.

High up, smoke still curled from the volcano, though the wind was starting to fray its edges. The glacier, a city of blue towers, the color of aquamarine just taken from the soil, squeezed between ruinous moraines. Three sheep, which had been grazing peacefully above the tree line, shot down the slope and fanned out—probably scared off by a fox. At the foot of the knoll, a meltwater creek ran between dark silt, ruffled into a waterfall, and then evened out again.

"Do you ever miss home?" Ulfar asked, gazing at the beauty around him.

"This is our home," Koll said.

"I know—but Norway."

"Where the king taxed us into the grave or open warfare? The loot robbed from us as soon as we robbed? The warlords and aristocrats? Never."

"But I mean the landscape, the towns and villages—our mothers? I think about your mother sometimes."

A look of pain crossed Koll's face.

"When I think of her, it's like a dagger in my heart, so I try not to."

There was silence. Sensing his friend's unwillingness to continue in that vein, Ulfar said, "Well, I'm hungry as a wolf."

Koll unslung a bag from around his shoulder. Inside it was bread, mushrooms, and dried mutton.

"I haven't eaten bread in a decade," Ulfar said. "I didn't know it would grow in this land."

"We have a little wheat and barley on my farm. They don't do well in this climate, but we are trying, and, as you'll see, not without success. I even have here a flask of ale, just for us."

Koll and Ulfar ate and drank for a while, quietly, happily. The plug of Yggdrasil's sap that had caught in Ulfar's throat was by now completely washed down, though its aftertaste lingered, adding a honeyed note to the fare. Ulfar dreamed of a better life, and for once his divorce and poverty didn't seem like such a bad thing. Perhaps the sap was working, as Koll said it would. He could rebuild his flock. He could build a new turf house. He could remarry and gain honor, inch by inch, as Koll had, and one day become a chief, even at this late age. But then the dark thoughts crowded in again, dimming the sap's glow. Of course it was no magical brew; that had been a silly fancy. How could he go about improving his life when his shame was broadcast to the world? His wife had divorced him, and then her brilliant father, the first great lawyer among the Icelanders, had stepped in to deprive Ulfar of his dowry, leaving him penniless and a laughingstock. Any strong man would have sought revenge, continued the feud at gatherings, and watched the night, sleepless, by the fire of his machinations. Ulfar's shame, however, had prevented any such recourse. He was impotent. He could not satisfy his wife. Though she was beautiful, he'd shrunk from her touch. What hurt him most was that he loved her—even now—but it was her character, her wisdom and humor, that he loved, not her tall, golden body.

"Look there," Koll said.

Ulfar snapped back to the reality around him. He didn't have to ask what Koll meant. It was plain to see. The creek below them had suddenly turned pink, silver, and brown as though a multi-colored cloud had formed atop the water. It was fish: dead salmon, turned on their sides and floating.

"Another sign from the gods," Koll said. "Your gifts grow, or my name isn't Koll Hognason. Let's boil some in that geyser pool we passed earlier. It's a wonderful way to cook salmon."

"I'll join you in a moment," Ulfar said. "My bladder is fit to burst."

Koll strode down the knoll to the creek. Ulfar took a piss, watching his friend's agile form leap over rocks.

Koll snatched up a salmon but then dropped it back in the water with a howl.

"The water's boiling!" he called.

As if in reply, the earth rumbled; the knoll quaked. Ulfar dove to the ground and held on to the thick moss for dear life. It was as though the knoll were a ship caught in a ferocious sea storm. Below, boiling creek water splashed onto Koll and he screamed. As the undulations became gentler and nearly petered out, Ulfar was on the verge of sprinting down to help his friend when the smoking volcano blew its cap, belching dark grey smoke and showering fiery boulders. The volcano was so high that they watched those orange boulders fall in slow motion from the heavens, taking a long, long time to hammer into the earth around them. The bigger blocks missed them, but a small, scalding meteorite lanced Ulfar's buttocks. He slapped the flames from his bloody skin and woolen trousers. Both friends stayed in place. They made eye contact, exchanging panic and confusion, but dared not stir. Lightning forked into a roiling ash cloud, part of which ascended into the stratosphere, the other part blasting evilly to the west, consuming the forests—fortunately away from them. Ash rained down, nevertheless, burning their eyes.

Again, the friends nearly stood up, thinking the act had reached its climax and that it was time to flee, when the earth rumbled a second time in the direction of the glacier; the blue towers, through the haze, collapsed and turned to seething mud, springing down the mountain towards them and the massive fragment of the world tree. There was no time. Koll ran three steps toward the knoll, and Ulfar ran three towards the creek, but the muddy torrent swept Koll away and he somersaulted underwater. The halberd rode the waves for a moment and then was sucked down as well.

Waves peaked around the knoll, splashing Ulfar with freezing water and then lava-hot water. Soon he would be drowned and flayed, like his friend. He couldn't quite believe this was happening. How could the world turn upside-down in a moment? A distant place in him suspected that this horror was indeed truth, and in that distant place a little boy wailed and cursed the heavens for his loss. Why Koll, the flower of talent and energy, and not him? As it was, though, the waves reared and flickered around the minor summit to which he clung, and he prayed to the gods for death to be swift and painless. Unlike Koll, he had no family or children to mourn him. That thought, amid the maelstrom, gave him some comfort and poise.

It had grown dark as dusk. A wave that Ulfar hadn't seen coming crashed against his legs and knocked him off his feet, but luckily not down the knoll. If the darkness didn't deceive him, the glacier was melting even more furiously, the mountain-high waterfall becoming more powerful as the minutes crept by. Being caught in this glacier leap in the gathering darkness, unable to see the huge, fatal wave that would overwhelm the knoll and invade his lungs, made his soul cower.

He couldn't take it any longer. He was about to find courage and jump down to join his old friend in a watery grave. Then, within the dark waterfall, backgrounded by orange lava gushing into the sky, a huge boulder or ice block dislodged from the glacier's bosom and rolled over, grey and rimmed with fire. But it was no boulder. It was the head of a giant. It floated away from the volcano toward Ulfar. Unlike the ice and pumice whizzing past him, this great head hovered, taking its time in its journey toward Ulfar, moving no faster than a longship with half its crew.

The glacier had calved and ejected the severed head of a god: one with ancient grey skin and wild red hair and a red beard, which trailed behind it like a comet's tail. The eye sockets were empty cavities. The mouth hung open, revealing teeth that were not teeth but golden rings embedded in dark gums. A small section of neck was intact, but ropes were coiled around it and hid the viscera where the blade—unimaginably large and sharp it must have been—had struck the neck. A decapitated and hanged god, a blind god: Odin or Mimir? Ulfar realized that Iceland, this gorgeous desert, must have been the very field of Ragnarök where the gods fought their final battles and died, pouring charmed blood into the ground. And here was proof. The gods lived no more. Ragnarök had come and gone. Ulfar and his Icelanders already lived in a future time.

Just as Ulfar arrived at this insight, the god's head sped up and struck the knoll with such force that he was thrown into the air and swallowed by the raging current.

ꝏ

Ulfar drowned over and over again. He resisted inhaling as long as possible, flailing about, and then his mouth opened involuntarily, his throat blazed, and water flooded his lungs. Impossibly, this kept happening. He'd wake in the burning and freezing currents, disoriented and blind and calling Koll's name. Then the drowning would recommence. At last he thudded against a bank of sharp rocks, vomiting water and blood. The flood had dragged him a few hundred yards away from the knoll and the volcano was partially hidden. As his panic and confusion lessened, he remembered gripping the god's beard and being hauled by it underwater until the head beached on a rocky shore. Ulfar wiped his eyes. There was no severed head in sight. Only rocks gouging his raw and skinless side and the muddy, ferocious, spontaneous river a few yards away, ripping through the valley, hazy in the ash fall.

He blacked out. When he awoke, Koll stood over him, water-logged, lips blue, and face half-flayed, missing large patches of skin. His creamy beard, reduced in size by the water to a thin icicle, had been dyed brown-grey and dripped glops of mud. One of his goatskin boots was missing, as were the expensive cloak and bronze brooch. Another phantom, Ulfar thought.

"I can't bear it," he rasped.

"You're a vision," Koll said.

"No, you are," Ulfar said. "You can't fool me. Go away."

His friend swarmed him, embracing him tightly and painfully and pressing his cold beard to his cheek.

"Thank the gods I found you. I despaired of it."

"You're a heavy vision," Ulfar said. He nearly blacked out again.

Koll shook him.

"We must leave. Now. We tied the horses not far from here. I've scouted a route up onto the plateau. We can't linger. The river will rise or there will be another explosion. I pray to the gods that the horses were not so frightened that they broke their bonds."

"Is it you?" Ulfar said, pawing at Koll's chest. "How is it possible?"

"Come," Koll said. He scooped Ulfar into his arms, gently standing him on his feet and steadying him with both hands.

"My friend," Ulfar gasped, falling into Koll's arms again. "You're alive? What happiness is this?" He pressed his face to Koll's neck. "And you stink. I've never known a vision to stink."

"Brother," Koll said tenderly, brushing wet hair from Ulfar's eyes. "There's no time. Gather your strength."

The friends limped up a steep gully onto the plateau. In the distance, the volcano raged, gushing lava. The sound it made wasn't so different from a heavy, rumbling wind. Surely the ash cloud billowed all the way to the sun. Lightning splintered yet thunder did not penetrate the volcano's roar.

They couldn't help but pause one final time at the plateau's edge.

"Where's the great branch?" Ulfar asked.

"Gone," Koll said.

Where Yggdrasil's limb had twisted up from the earth, the glacial flood, along with what appeared to be a landslide, had buried it; that remnant of magical existence had vanished, like most others. The branch was now inaccessible.

Ulfar's heart sank and his eyes watered. He had always doubted the stories of the gods yet told these doubts to no one; he'd made sacrifices and whittled effigies like everyone else. And now he knew that the ancient stories were true, or that they had been. This present world was a barrow of relics atop which people danced.

"The Æsir and Vanir are dead," Ulfar announced. "They have been dead for a long time. Ragnarök has come and gone. We live in a future time and the world, long ago, was born anew."

"What are you saying? You're ill. But no matter, so am I. My head spins and my body burns and water still sloshes in my lungs. None of it makes sense. How did we survive that horror? Did that draught from Yggdrasil's branch cause this calamity or prove our salvation? Yech, no time for this. The forest isn't two miles away. I recognize this place. Hurry, we must hurry."

ଋ

They passed through what seemed to be an endless field of thyme, the spring colors dimmed by ash, until they arrived at the forest. By this time the brown sun sat atop the mountains. Their horses frothed at the mouth and blinked the ash from their eyes.

After a few miles at a flying pace, they reached Ulfar's sagging turf house and cared for the horses with hay and water.

"We are not safe yet," Koll said. "Gather your things. Ride south with me."

"What about your meeting with that chief, Ore-Bjorn of Bjarnardale? You made it seem so important."

"Obviously that can wait. Ride south with me. Alf will welcome you—she is a fierce yet loving woman and honors guests. But you'll be more than a guest. I don't care what anyone says or thinks. You'll live with us. You'll stay close to me. I can't part with you again. Even more than our boyhoods, this event has bound us for life. We are fated to brave this world side by side."

Ulfar gathered his things silently for a while. He'd love nothing more than to be beside his friend day and night, in blizzards and at lambing time, under northern lights and during the sheep shearing season, to have Koll there to hold him when he had nightmares of that family burning alive in the farmhouse. But all that was impossible now. He would have to find a middle ground.

"Back there," Ulfar said, "on death's margin, I was given knowledge. Sacred knowledge. I know it is blasphemous, but I saw a sight, a severed and floating god's head that told me, wordlessly but emphatically, that the gods have slaughtered each other and that there's no future for us on Valhalla's mead benches or even in Hel. I must spread this news abroad. I will winter with you; I love you and cannot be parted from you either, not for long. But when the springtime comes, I must wander this land and impart my knowledge, come what may. It will be a dangerous mission. I see that you want to speak those words to me. That it isn't wise; that men will resist and harm me. Well, it isn't wise. I'm not mad. Yggdrasil's sap gave me second sight and now that its branch is lost under water and rock, I am like a remnant of that great tree loose on the earth."

"Can there be hope in godlessness?" Koll asked quietly.

Ulfar lit a lamp of shark oil. The men changed into dry clothes; they had been dangerously close to frostbite without realizing it. Ulfar shoved a handful of lichen into his mouth and gave some to Koll, as well as a blackened field mouse on a stick. Chewing with the grit and ash in their mouths was like eating tiny, bitter crystals, and they drank as much water as they could handle.

"There is hope for me," Ulfar said at last. "And maybe for others. They will call me Ulfar the Godless. Many will jeer; a few will listen. All my sacrifices have yielded only pain and regret. This is my new beginning." He paused and smiled. Just because he had found a calling didn't mean he'd neglect the pleasures of life—no, not with this newfound confidence; so he added, "By the way, do you want to hear a joke about an ugly chieftain and a handsome peasant?"

Koll brightened up. He gave Ulfar's beard a little tug. "Now that's a message I want to hear."

The Cloud Dungeon

The sisters, Osk and Idunn, loaded their boat with stolen sheep and pushed off. The boat slithered across the black sand and wobbled into the icy surf, awkward with the unaccustomed weight. Freezing slush splattered the sheep, who yelled and croaked and burped with wide, trembling eyes. The sisters' island, about a mile from the shore, rose like a green shark's fin from the sea, and despite being engulfed in shuffling wool, they rowed the distance speedily.

It was midwinter and barely enough grey light remained for them to haul the sheep onto the craggy beach. They had made the most of the five hours of daylight—robbing the sheep pens of the prominent farmer whose son, who lived in the east, had been killed by an axe blow to the brain, and whose burial mound and funeral rites the farmer had left to attend to.

Idunn was the oldest and tallest, twenty-one and six-foot-five. Osk was nineteen and a mere six-foot-two. They both had dark skin and golden hair, and if it weren't for the height difference, no one could tell them apart. They worked so synchronously that they hadn't spoken since loading the sheep onto the boat.

Their island was an isolated tower, moated by tumultuous waves and icebergs, so they didn't bother glancing behind them to see if any farmhands had followed. They guided the ewes up the rough-hewn steps that, midway up the cliff, flattened out to a shelf with a cavemouth. Here they had made a humble home with a sleeping bench and an open hearth, whose smoke drifted to a small hole in the cave's roof. In the summer, there would be enough grass on the slopes to feed the sheep, but they had stores enough to keep the livestock alive until then. The cave would be warm with all the animal bodies, and though it would turn nasty with turds and piss, they could endure filth, thankful they didn't have to clean it up if they didn't feel like it.

"That was almost too easy," Idunn said once they'd revived the fire, inflaming the eyes of the sheep.

"Maybe we shouldn't plan things out so carefully next time," Osk said, "if it's action you want."

"Let's consider that, certainly," her sister said.

They dipped their gold-inlaid drinking horns in a bucket of amber liquid and toasted each other.

"To you, sister."

"No, to you."

They sat for a while in silence, grinning slightly, reveling in the warmth.

A green flame of the northern lights lapped the cavemouth. How swiftly the darkness fell in winter! Both watched the weave of light on rock, mesmerized by it as it shifted colors from green to blue to green; very gradually, an orange-reddish glow bled into it. At first, the sisters thought nothing of this new addition, merely admiring a rare variation of the aurora's color palette, but then glanced at each other quickly, questioningly, and darted to the cavemouth.

Outside, the meandering northern lights revealed a shadowy boat on the beach and a dim figure, torch in hand, climbing the steps of their crag. They examined the ocean and near-distant mainland for signs of reinforcements, but there were none: only this solitary boat and figure.

"What madness would lead him to venture here alone?" Idunn whispered, her breath pluming with cold.

"Maybe a shepherd," Osk mused, "come to beg us for his beloved flock? I suppose we've stolen someone's animal friends—some old tender heart. It couldn't be helped."

"But it's well below freezing now. Who would brave those bergs and waves on such a bitter evening? Why not wait until morning to get revenge, if that's what he wants? It's either a cocky warrior seeking adventure and bragging rights or a distraught shepherd, as you say."

"Well, let's prepare," Osk said. "Perhaps we'll have some action after all."

They gathered their swords from their little armory. Idunn preferred fighting with a long sword, its hilt ornately designed with a bronze bear, while Osk fought with two simple iron short swords. They snuck out of the cave and took their positions behind two boulders that served as perfect spots for surprise attacks, which they'd practiced many times together on rainy days when there was nothing much to do on the crag but eat and ponder the dull ocean.

The torch brightened. The footsteps, shuffling and slow, became louder.

Soon firelight spread across the rock shelf. The hooded figure paused, turning this way and that.

The sisters sprang from their hiding places, and before there was even time for an exclamation, the point of Idunn's long sword prodded the man's belly, while Osk's short swords were crossed like shears, each blade touching his neck, which a quick snip could turn headless.

"Drop the torch," Idunn said.

"One little move and your head flies."

The torch plummeted to the ground and rolled to the cliff's edge, the flame guttering.

"Now what do you want?" Osk asked.

"Quick with it! We don't like trespassers."

The hood was thrown back, revealing a sharp and angular face, grotesquely blistered; a woman's face with hungry eyes, neither young nor old with hair, if the guttering flame and northern lights didn't lie, the color of muted amethyst, that swirled around her scalp like a pile of crystal dung. Her pupils were black, the anxious, all-consuming black of the deep underground.

"The sister thieves?" the woman asked. Her accent was archaic, that of their grandmother in Norway, but also with a tinge of something else, perhaps the Saxon tongue; her voice was very dry as if she hadn't drunk water for days. "A pleasure to meet you. I come with business."

The sisters relaxed a little, though they didn't lower their weapons. Inside the cave, there was a brief chorus of baas.

"It's forbidden to come to the Island of the Sister Thieves without penalty," Osk said.

"Quite a fancy name for this heap of rock," the woman said.

Osk re-tightened her shears on the woman's neck.

"Let's hear what the ugly hag has to say," Idunn said. "If it sounds the least bit tricksy, we'll sport with her head, see how far we can kick it into the ocean."

"I offer riches," the woman said.

From her cloak she brandished a pendant of rock crystal and a golden arm ring, offering them to the sisters, one object in each hand. Idunn and Osk glanced at the treasures but didn't move.

"Continue," they said in unison.

"As you can see, even in this mild darkness, I am mutilated by the sun. I am one of the hid-folk. An exile in the bright regions. Until a year ago, I lived with my kinsfolk in a mountain your people call Trullafell. From your perspective it would be a wondrous mountain. May I keep going?"

The sisters nodded.

"This mountain is wondrous because within it, a mile underground, resides a cloud. We call this cloud Ix. It is holy and older than the mountain itself. We worship it, feed on its thick, creamy, floating crystals, at once heavy as skyr and light as a wafer: there's simply nothing like it.

"I was charged with gluttony and outlawed. They said that I overate of the cloud. I could not get enough of its vital slush, and I'd eat when no one was looking. To hid-folk, Ix is the most toothsome milk on the planet, and it was as if I contained ten of my kinsfolk inside me, so great was my greed for it. So they barred me from Trullafell forever, saying my gluttony was an affront to the laws. Since then, I have cowered under upper world rocks and slept in barrows of the dead, eating unwholesome mushrooms and avoiding the sunlight, but always discovered by it and mutilated. Your sun is cruel, persistent.

"So, what does this have to do with you? I can no longer enter my home. The spells against me are too strong; believe me, I have tried. But you can enter. And I ask you to do two things: trap some of the cloud in a special container I shall provide, and then free Ix from its mountain hold and let it fly into the heavens, where it was meant to be, and thus take revenge on those who exiled me. I offer these two gifts as down payments; at a barrow, I have treasures that shall be yours as well: rings and coins and pendants and goblets and swords and golden halberds."

"Golden halberds?" Idunn asked, a little flustered with desire.

"Shush now," Osk said. "Let's consider this practically. Can you prove, woman, that you are indeed one of the hid-folk? I've heard they have lavender blood."

"This is true," the woman said.

"Cut her, Idunn."

Idunn released a hand from her long sword, and despite its weight, her muscular right arm held the sword firm. From her belt she withdrew a knife.

"Place the pendant and ring down at your feet," Idunn said. "That's it. Move slowly. Now hold out your arm."

In a flash Idunn pulled up a sleeve and sliced the woman's pale grey arm. Blood beaded from the wound.

"Are you in control of the situation, sister?" Idunn asked. "I must get light."

"Of course," Osk said.

Idunn walked to the cliff's edge and picked up the woman's guttering torch. She brought it over and held the fire an inch above the wound, which indeed branched with lavender blood.

"Believe me?" the woman said with a smile.

The sisters exchanged glances. Idunn checked the woman's cloak for weapons or vials of poison but found nothing; she picked up the pendant and arm ring. Osk lowered her twin swords.

"Well...welcome to our home, stranger; we don't have much to offer in the way of hospitality except warmth and mead. What shall we call you?"

"They call me Fogrest."

"Fogrest?" Idunn asked. "What kind of name is that?"

"A hid-folk name, a mountain name," the woman said coldly.

"A fine name," Osk said. "Come inside and tell us more. If the adventure is worthy of a poet's song, free of folly and no wild goose chase, our decision might be in your favor. But that's to be seen."

☙

In the cave, the woman drew a map on a patch of black sand. It showed the rivers, valleys, and icefields one would have to cross to reach Trullafell, and the secret entrance to the mountain. When the sisters expressed dismay at the length and resources required for such a journey and a growing reluctance, Fogrest gave them the two gold-and-amber rings on her fingers, which contained little flies inside them—worth twice all the sheep they had just stolen.

"How can we be sure you're not lying?" Osk asked. "That you don't want to trick us? That there won't be a legion of hid-folk waiting for us at this secret door, ready to chop us into steak?"

"What would my motive be? Burn my boat if you want. Trap me on your island. I don't mind. I'll watch your sheep while you're gone. No men in this region are as skilled as you two at thieving. Your cleverness has been broadcast far and wide. For my revenge, I can trust no others. Now that I have seen you with my own eyes, I believe that even more."

The sisters couldn't help feeling flattered, though Idunn seemed more eager than Osk to enter into a contract with the stranger. Osk could almost see the golden halberd glittering in her sister's eyes.

"Do we need her supposed riches?" Osk said. "We are rich in the stuff that matters in this land—sheep and mead and a beautiful prospect."

"Come, sister," Idunn said. "Enough of scruples. This is an opportunity to sit on a treasure hoard like a dragon and never worry about anything ever again. We deserve this chance."

Suddenly Fogrest shoved her hand into the fire. It happened so quickly that the sisters didn't know how to react. The hand flickered and smoked, pervading the cave with the smell of cooked meat before Idunn tackled the woman, forcing her hand from the flames. It was swollen and oozing.

"I swear on my life," Fogrest gasped. "I do not lie. Bring me a horn-full of the cloud and release it from the mountain, and I'll give you everything. Please, great sisters"—she groveled—"help me take my revenge. It is an honest revenge. Everything I love has been stolen from me."

The sisters couldn't help but respect Fogrest's courage.

"We accept," Idunn said. "Right, little sister?"

Osk shrugged. "I suppose. It seems reckless, but I'd like to see a mountain's heart. And if it'll make you happy..."

"It will," Idunn said, smiling, her teeth yellow as butter. "I want a challenge for once, something to trouble our waters. I'm sick of robbing petty farmers." She turned back to

Fogrest. "One thing you still haven't explained. How do we free the cloud from the mountain?"

"Ah, now that's easier than you might think," Fogrest whispered, blowing on her mangled hand and shedding tears uncontrollably. "But it is something a human would never imagine."

ଓ

The next morning, they took the massive horn from Fogrest's skiff (the drinking vessel was made of a substance shiny and pliable like mica and allegedly able to trap wisps of cloud) and set off for the mainland, shouting instructions to Fogrest concerning the sheep and protection of the island. She simply bowed her head. The sisters couldn't help but trust her after the previous night's display.

They hid their boat in a small mainland cave but fully expected it to be found and stolen. The rock crystal pendant around Idunn's neck, the arm ring clasping Osk's bicep, and the amber rings they both wore on their pinky fingers could buy twenty such rowboats.

They stole two hardy stallions—wounded from horse fighting and a little skittish but overall strong and happy for a new situation—from an outlying farm and galloped over the thin layer of snow blanketing the land near the ocean. As they moved farther into the interior, the horses fell flank-deep in the drifts, and they had to steal a sleigh from a large man on the way to a wrestling match; upon hearing their names (the much-feared Idunn and Osk) he stopped cursing and resisting, and even graciously smoothed down the furs on the sleigh's bed and pointed them to the Lake of Wool, which would be the halfway mark of their journey, thirty miles northeast.

The sisters traveled through bitter cold and under the oxbows of the northern lights, Orion's glittering belt and bent bow, and the half-light of the moon; in blind conditions when the snow drove and in the freezing rain, which, as any traveler knows, is the most dangerous enemy of all.

On a blue, stormless day, the sisters whiled away the time with conversation, which the conditions had thwarted up until then. They glided alongside the Lake of Wool, where, according to legend, a thousand sheep had once drowned, driven into it by some sudden madness. The waters never froze even at midwinter but were yellow-brown like rotten wool, the weird surf ever sucking up and down the beach. Osk and Idunn, a bit uneasy, whetted their swords.

Osk said, "I wonder what Bergfinn and Kvist would say if they knew their wives were passing the infamous Lake of Wool, alone at midwinter."

"They'd call us fools but not to our faces," Idunn said.

Osk laughed. "Certainly not. But they'd disappear to the privy, carrying kettles of porridge, and gossip their heads off. I couldn't stand the way they'd eat food while taking shits."

"They were unsanitary cowards, that's for sure."

"I wish I felt worse about them dying," Osk said. "I wondered if my feelings would change, but I still feel relief, contentment—no nostalgia, nothing."

"Why should you feel different? We didn't love them."

"No, we didn't," Osk continued, "but still, I wish they'd died memorably—in a way that we could at least joke about or fight over. You can't start a feud over drowning. They were good enough men to revenge if someone had been decent enough to murder them."

"Yes, they were good enough for that," Idunn said, her voice a little sad despite herself. "You never composed a poem about them," she went on reflectively. "Did they deserve that honor?"

"I don't know," Osk said. "I suppose there's time to come up with a poem. Do you want to help me?"

"You know I have no gift for that kind of thing. When we release this cloud and claim our reward, perhaps I'll throw a silver coin into the sea for them—something's better than nothing. I sometimes wonder if the gods are displeased at our heartlessness. It's been what—two years?"

"I think so," Osk said. "But if anything, the gods are displeased with your greed. You've mentioned that golden halberd too many times."

"Not that again, sister," Idunn said. "You promised to stop nagging me about wanting a few nice things to fill our cavern and improve our armory—some security for our long lives. If you didn't want to come on this journey, you didn't have to agree. I didn't force you. Compose your poem and leave me be."

Osk sighed. "Fine, fine. A truce. I'll drop it for now. I'm as keen for adventure as you, though the spoils entice me less. And maybe in another five years I'll forget enough of the unpleasant things about marriage to feel inspired to write a poem about our late husbands. That's how memory works, eh? Time scrapes out the rot. As of now, I'm still too relieved they're gone."

ᘓ

At last, after a precarious journey over an icefield, Trullafell pushed its green nose from the earth.

The sisters found an overhanging rock where their horses could feed on a bag of oats and avoid the worst of any inclement weather. They left the horses there without tying them up; a trust had grown between the four of them since the beasts had never had such caring masters before. The sisters unpacked the sleigh. Idunn slung Fogrest's massive drinking horn, big as a troll's horn, across her back, and Osk fastened a fox-skin pouch of kindling and other useful items around her waist; the older sister propped her bear-hilted long sword on her shoulder and the younger sheathed her short swords in a thong contraption strapped to her back, ready to draw at any moment.

The mountain was so steep that most of its mossy sides were snowless and covered in rime, which silvered the green; deep snowpack only loaded the summit and gashes in the cliffs. They thanked the gods that the hidden door wasn't at the summit; climbing a nearly vertical volcanic cone with the winds racing across the adjacent icefields would be a task they could certainly accomplish, but not without much unpleasantness. The hidden door, Fogrest had said, was near the mountain's base and directly behind a tiny, inconsequential waterfall, like someone overturning a washing tub.

Within an hour they found a waterfall that fit the description. They trekked up a gully, black sand and pebbles pouring into their boots. They peered behind the veil of water and icicles and found a hole in the rock, no bigger than a fist. It was hard to believe it was the entrance.

"That woman will make fools of us yet," Osk said.

Idunn patted the crystal pendant around her neck. "Hid-folk rules don't correspond to our own. You know that. Some of the tales Father told us have already turned out true. The lavender blood, for instance. Stop wasting time doubting and stay close to me. Don't lose your swords in the passage."

"Go on," Osk said. "Show the way."

Idunn touched the edge of the tiny vent, which a rabbit could hardly squeeze through. She put her hand inside the cool darkness, then her arm, which didn't seem like it would fit. She lowered her head and prepared to meet rock. Instead, it passed through easily, without touching the vent's edges, and her eyes, as they adjusted to the dimness, found themselves in a tunnel high and wide enough to stand in. She brought the rest of her body through without her long sword or the great drinking horn hitting anything. Fogrest hadn't lied. Here was a magic door, known only to the hid-folk, that few humans would ever notice or consider entering.

Osk, seeing her sister disappear through the tiny vent, couldn't help but follow. On the other side, the tunnel expanded, but the pale door behind them, by some illusion, still looked a fist's size.

After walking a few yards, the outside light leaked away. Idunn and Osk inched forward. They couldn't light a torch, not yet. The hid-folk could smell smoke and pitch from a mile away. Any fire lit in the underground was, Fogrest had informed them, restricted to sealed chambers. Plus, they knew that at the end of this tunnel stood a guard, whom they must dispatch quietly in the dark.

As they moved along, minerals like chips of silver began to populate the surrounding rocks, reminding them of the stars at night and gently illuminating the passage. They had never encountered phosphorescent minerals before. What were they? Idunn scratched one hard chip of light with her fingernail, wondering if it had any value. Her sister nudged her forward.

Up ahead, if their eyes didn't deceive them, the tunnel ended. They stood still and listened. The guard—their first obstacle—must be near. They could hear nothing at first. But when they held their breath at the same time, very distantly, a rattling noise sawed through the silence, rising and falling. They crept forward, unsheathing their swords. The tunnel brightened ever so slightly with an arc of blue light. They peeked around a corner, and there he was, armored in a semi-transparent mineral like mica, his visor tilted to his chest, snoring; a crystal spear leaned against the rock wall beside him. It seemed that the guard's post was more ceremonial than precautionary.

Idunn leaped forward and drove her sword through a vulnerable point in the guard's neck. He stopped snoring and gurgled; his body spasmed. Lavender blood trickled down the blade.

"We could have gagged him and tied him up," Osk said reflectively. "You didn't have to kill him; he was sound asleep."

"Don't be naïve," Idunn said. "You're starting to annoy me. Let's just find that staircase."

☙

Chips of phosphorescent silver peppered the cavern. As they moved along a flat expanse of rock, Osk noticed runes carved into the walls, thousands upon thousands of them, some in shadow, others glittering. She paused to marvel at them, wishing she could read them. What were hid-folk stories like? Hid-folk beliefs? She knew so little about their culture. Idunn shot her an impatient look but allowed her sister a few moments to take in the thousand-foot walls chiseled with runes from top to bottom.

"Maybe it's a long poem?" Osk wondered aloud. "About a hid-folk warrior? One day I'll ask some wise witch to teach me the secrets of reading and writing. That would make me happier than any raid."

"I think you're a hid-folk in disguise," Idunn muttered.

"Eat sheep's head," Osk said.

"Gladly," Idunn said. "You know how I relish the eyes."

Towards the cliff's rim, the silver-blue glow intensified. They crawled over to the edge. And what they saw astounded even Idunn. A hollow mountain, miles wide and nearly a mile deep. Down below, perhaps four thousand feet, a cloud lay at anchor. Here, at long last, was their quarry. The cloud resembled a thunderhead. Encircling the cloud, along the cavern's perimeter, was a band of trees littered with luminous mineral chips. An underground forest whose trees must be thick as giants' legs, but from the sisters' giddy height were no more than sparkling briars.

Ix, as Fogrest had called the cloud, was like a dark hill in the forest's center. As they gazed, it seemed to shift, to boil for a few seconds, then to freeze, as if caught in an unseemly act, only to shift and boil again.

Among the trees hid-folk milled about, tiny as gnats from the sisters' vantage point. The hid-folk seemed to take pains to avoid entering the cloud, keeping to the trees on the perimeter. Idunn spotted a staircase cut into the cliffside. They must sneak down it. Fogrest claimed the population of this cavern did not exceed sixty hid-folk, which complicated their mission without making it as dangerous as raiding a typical human settlement.

They crept down the stairs, zigzagging across the cliff face. A few figures paused below and seemed to gaze up at them; the sisters froze. But soon enough the figures moved on and disappeared into the trees. About halfway down the cliff, they drew level with the top of the cloud, which boiled ferociously and stilled into smooth cream. It was as if not only the hollow mountain imprisoned the cloud, but the forest itself acted as a tight belt, with the cloud gathering strength and lashing out for freedom; then, the battle lost, it was squeezed into submission once again. The cloud, even to their unrefined human noses, emitted the tantalizing scent of chilled curds and the floral notes of mountain avens, making their mouths water. If their eyes didn't deceive them, it was about a half mile away. First, they must reach ground level and pass through the forest.

When they reached the stair's end and eased down onto a root fruiting with dark mushrooms, a flash of lightning spurted past them and struck the stairs. The lightning bolt shivered in the rock. No thunder followed, however. It was no lightning bolt, after all, but a crystal spear.

A horn blew, then another, and another, echoing through the cavern. Cries erupted, eerie cries, full of fear and despair.

"Go!" Idunn whispered.

"Keep the stairs in sight," Osk said. "Don't lose your way."

"Same to you, sister. Stay oriented; I can't do without you."

They sprinted into the trees, but soon Idunn, heading in a straight line, outstripped her sister; Osk turned aside to one of the great trunks, large enough to fit a house in—and indeed, the hollow tree seemed to be the living quarters of hid-folk, full of glittering furniture and a blue, luminescent boulder in the room's center. A hid-folk, huffing like a bear, with grey skin and long amethyst hair, lifted as from static, suddenly blocked the entrance to this tree. Another crystal spear flew past Osk's face. She ducked and scrambled towards a different trunk.

Osk needed to find a hollow tree empty of hid-folk: that was her aim. Their numbers had fallen over the last century, the sisters had been told, so there should be plenty of trees no longer lived in; and if Osk couldn't locate an abandoned domicile, she'd need to empty it herself, though she hated to commit more violence after the guard's murder. One death was enough.

Once inside a tree, she'd light her torch and set it ablaze. The soft, flammable insides of the trees, unlike the outside bark spangled with hard minerals, would catch fire easily, and if one great tree burst into flame, its fury would penetrate the surrounding trees despite their coats of armor. With the forest aflame, its squeeze on the cloud would weaken, and the cloud would rise, rootle its way out of the mountain dungeon, out of the smallest chink, and flee to the sky.

The huffing noises continued behind Osk. The hid-folk woman with lifted hair, and some of her kith and kin, trailed Osk, close on her heels. She ran faster, turned into a narrow gap between two colossal trees, dove under a root, and scrambled through a woody archway.

ᘓ

Meanwhile, Idunn neared the cloud. An arrow whooshed and nicked her nose. She leaped over a stream, which seemed to pour over a bed of stars, and pressed on, passing a final tree before the dark wall of cloud rose before her. Ahead, in the false moonlight of the underground, a hid-folk, undeterred by the horn blasts and cries and flying darts, gathered wisps of Ix into her hands, which she pressed to her mouth. She repeated this act, gathering and pressing. She gasped and fell to her knees, trembling with pleasure. The heavy incense of cream and flowers filled Idunn's nostrils.

"Gloomy fires of Ix," the woman cried in an accent matching Fogrest's. "Runes of the earth! Beard of the cosmos! Listen to me, your priestess. Protect us!"

Idunn plunged her blade into the priestess's back. She kicked the woman's body—thrashing wildly like a poet performing for a king—face-first into the cloud; she fell into its dark wool up to the waist, looking like she'd been cut in two. Runes were tattooed across her bare feet.

Remembering herself, Idunn unstrapped the drinking horn from her back and dragged it through the cloud. She peered inside doubtfully, but the drinking horn was full, somehow trapping the dark mist inside it. The air swirled and bubbled without spilling over the horn's lip.

Fogrest's sacred brew. One half of her revenge. It wouldn't be long before the sisters' island became a treasure chest for Arabic coins, precious rings fashioned by dwarves and, topping it all off, a golden halberd, the likes of which no warrior had ever seen. Now Osk simply needed to set fire to a tree and this underground world would burn spectacularly, its cloud prisoner set free. The sisters would be powerful beyond measure and could live a life of ease.

Idunn licked the cloud herself. She was disappointed. She'd expected a skyr-thick, clotted morsel, but for her—for humans, she supposed—it could not whet the palate, warm the belly, ignite pleasure. It was empty, flavored air. She licked again. Yes, it was pleasant but not succulent.

Just then, a crystal spear skewered her shoulder, and her long sword clanged to the ground.

☙

Flames licked up the walls of a large tree room, spiraling towards the heartwood. Osk dropped the torch and, amid desperate cries and billowing smoke, rushed out of the hollow just as a party of three hid-folk, armored in minerals like the guard Idunn had slain, closed in on her. All three hid-folk paused for a split second when they saw the smoke billowing from the tree.

"Water!" one cried.

"Water or our doom!" cried another.

These two turned, flailing and hollering, into the woods—presumably toward water. However, the largest of these three mineral knights, a bear, it seemed, standing upright and disguised in hid-folk panoply, charged Osk, a blue-glowing sword hoisted above his head.

Osk parried his arcing attack and struck a glancing blow in return. The knight, a demon coated in crystal, a berserker unlike any Osk had ever fought, bore down on her with reckless abandon, roaring and swinging with fearful power, each of his strikes furious, desperate, inspired. She couldn't help but retreat slightly. Where was her sister? Where were the stairs? She had failed to stay oriented. She cursed herself and this vain, idiotic quest. They'd raze this hid-folk city and die in the process. As the sword rained down, iron biting iron and her own blades cracking, she swore, if the gods were watching and she escaped this debacle, to leave behind thievery and mercenary work. Very likely, that would mean leaving her sister, too.

Behind the combatants the flames lengthened. The fire spread to the outer bark of the great tree where its phosphorescent chips sizzled and popped, their lights extinguished but replaced by the bloodier blaze. A fireball flickered along a branch and jumped to another tree.

Shadows, carrying basins of splashing water, appeared, frantic to reach the fire's source. The heat mounted. Embers showered upon them. Now a second treetop burned.

The berserker's sword sliced off the nub of Osk's elbow. She crumpled, howling.

His blade shattered both Osk's swords; it felt like the ligaments had snapped in her palms and her wrists had fractured. She looked up into the black, seething eyes in the visor's slit. If she weren't in such pain, so winded and half-dead, she would have told him she was sorry. She tried to communicate that message through her half-open eyes. At least she would perish at the hands of a great warrior, worthy of a thousand rune poems. In her mind she said goodbye to her sister.

Hid-folk swarmed around them, dumping water into the conflagration.

"Leave off, Algarot!"

"Forget the human; we'll meet her in Hel or in the upper world. We need more hands!"

"Help us, Algarot!"

The berserker paused, the point of his sword touching the ground behind him, ready for a brutal swing. He released it and said, "A curse on you and a curse on Fogrest. We know who sent you."

"Give us," Osk mumbled, unable to articulate the 'for' in the first word. Did the hid-folk warrior know what she meant, understand her regret, or did he think her greed so ravenous that even now she wanted the hid-folk to give more: their cloud, their forest, their riches, their world?

"A curse on you," the berserker repeated.

Just as he turned towards where his fellow hid-folk had come, lugging water, the atmosphere changed and there was a marked shift in pressure.

A tongue of cloud lifted above the trees.

Fifty-odd voices, all at once, cried some version of *no*.

The tongue of cloud rose higher then stopped, hovering over the flames.

"Ix is breaking free, taking flight!" someone shrieked.

"The transmutation!"

Osk, clutching her streaming, maimed elbow, stumbled in the opposite direction from the cloud, presumably toward the cliff wall. Idunn's task, filling Fogrest's horn with the cloud, had been more straightforward, so she had probably reached the staircase and was waiting there. Osk wove between the trunks, almost all of which—how could it happen so quickly?—ran with flames; branches cascaded down, so Osk had to keep an eye on the situation above as well as in front of her.

She nearly collided face-first into the cliff. She passed her hand over its crinkled rock thankfully, looking left and right for the stairs. Panic, however, began to eat into her relief. If she chose the wrong direction, she could get lost again or have another confrontation with a hid-folk warrior; and how much time would it take to escape? The heat was becoming almost unbearable. On a hunch, she chose right and, running her fingers along the twinkling minerals and mysterious runes, eventually met the hewn stone of the staircase.

But Idunn wasn't there.

Osk waited and waited. Smoke stung her eyes. A flaming leaf landed on her hair, turning its gold to embers before she snuffed it.

There was no choice; she had to leave without her sister. She scurried up the stairs. After about a hundred steps, she tripped over something. A body with a crystal spear lodged in it. A shifting body. A hid-folk? She jumped over it.

"Osk?" Idunn whimpered, her hand outstretched. "Come back."

"Idunn? You left without me?"

"And you without me."

"I had no choice," Osk said.

"Nor did I. Never mind all that. Help me remove this splinter from my shoulder. It's heavy. I can't walk with it inside me."

ଊ

In each other's bloody arms, the sisters eventually attained the high shelf with the slain guard and secret door. By now Ix had broken its anchorage and hovered in its entirety, a dark floating hill above the burning trees, half-obscuring the flames below. The cloud had risen thousands of feet. It seemed to follow the sisters, gliding towards the door.

"It worked," Idunn said, gazing at the cloud. "We've accomplished the mission. We'll be rich."

"Not if we're dead."

"Always the pessimist."

"If the cloud overtakes us, we won't be able to find the door. We'll have to search for it blindly and may fall off the cliff, back down to those poor hid-folk. Don't talk again until we're outside. You'll jinx us."

Osk drew her sister forward and they passed through the door. The cloud stretched a finger after them. It wriggled into the tunnel, gaining speed. It was no longer redolent of chilled curds and aspens but charcoal and scorched flesh and lightning. It had become grimly ecstatic, feral.

The sisters stumbled out of the magical vent in the mountain into the outside world, drenched by the cold waterfall and slaked with fresh air. For the first time Osk noticed that Fogrest's horn was still strapped to Idunn's back and full of grey mist.

The great cloud curled out of the vent, too, probing the ground. It then shot out, gushing, eddying, gaining mass, a thunderhead accumulating behind the sisters as they hobbled down the gully.

When Ix had gathered its entire body, it floated upwards.

Desperate cries spilled from the door in the mountain. The sisters, almost at the gully's bottom, turned around. Hid-folk, likewise burnt and half-naked, scrambled through the waterfall, hands clawing at the cloud, trying in vain to skim even the slightest morsel into their palms, but the cloud was already ten feet above them. They stampeded over each other, praying and pleading for Ix to return. They cried out that they loved it; without it, they had no hearth and home; without it, they'd leap off the mountain. They cried *stop* and *please* and *help* and *no* and *a curse on Fogrest and the human thieves*. Even the berserker Algarot, now shorn of his armor, wept like a deserted lover and raised his muscular arms in vain, his amethyst beard all but burnt away.

The cloud changed shapes as it glided up the mountainside, as if experimenting with new bodies, new dresses. It flattened into a disc, spun into a tornadic tube, and plumped into an ungainly shape like a dwarf on a horse. When hid-folk clambered up the slopes, seeing that the cloud had not strayed far from the rocks and hoping for the briefest contact with it, Ix backed away from the mountain, just enough, so that an arrow could penetrate it but no creature touch it.

The cloud drifted up and up. When it finally overtook Trullafell's summit, it transformed from a storm cloud into a white, nondescript cumulus cloud, fluffy and towering—for, after all, it was a beautiful winter day. It sailed towards the setting sun, low in the sky.

ꝏ

The sisters readied their horses—somewhat awkwardly, each using only one arm—and skidded away on the sled. The surviving hid-folk became dots on the mountainside. No one pursued them.

When Trullafell was hidden behind another mountain, Idunn said, "Let's clean our wounds in the snow up ahead. You see that bank? I bet there's water, too."

"Yes," Osk said weakly.

Idunn kissed her sister's dirty forehead. "We're rich."

"You're rich."

"What did you say?"

"How could riches be on your mind right now? After what happened?"

"We're shield-maidens, bereft of husbands and fending for ourselves and our independence. I'm happy to pay any price. And what an adventure it was! I thought you wanted adventure?"

"Not like that," Osk said. "I don't know if I can live with myself."

"Don't be a weakling, little sister. I thought I beat that out of you long ago."

"I can't unsee the burning," Osk said, lost in thought. "Unhear the cries. The curses."

"We're victorious. We'll live on a mound of riches. I'm surprised at you. You lose a bit of elbow and you lose your nerve."

"I'm leaving," Osk said. "When we get to the crossroads."

"The hell you are."

"We've murdered a world," Osk whispered.

"I'm getting you to a healer. Your brain's addled."

"Before we reach the crossroads on the far side of the Lake of Wool," Osk said, "I'll compose a poem for you and your heroics. One that celebrates your gift to Fogrest, and her bestowal of unimaginable riches upon you. If you desire followers, you'll become an earl. If you desire solitude, you'll become a dragon. But I must also compose poems for the hid-folk and seek their forgiveness, somehow make up for some of this, impossible as that is. No compensation can ever be paid for that cloud or those lives. But I'll do what I can. And if you try to stop me, as I see is your intent, I'll kill myself before you get the chance. I swear it by the gods."

Idunn sat there, stunned.

Far away, high above the frozen ocean, a long-lost cloud entered the night.

Eldgrim

I first knew something was wrong when the father did not strip naked. He held a torch aloft, as was the custom, and walked towards the boat where his son lay dead, but he made no move to take off his clothes and no one, to my amazement, said or did anything. I glanced at Eldgrim the Priest, expecting him to intervene, but he just stood there in his white cloak, brandishing his staff, chanting prayers for the dead.

It was late autumn, cold, and snowing a little, the night slightly fuzzed with it, but that was no excuse to ignore the rites. The gods see all, hear all, even wool growing. I trembled at the divine retribution that would follow if the father did not strip naked before reaching the funereal boat.

I shifted position. I couldn't help it. A few drops of blood sloshed out of the bowl I was holding.

Eldgrim shot me an angry look. His blue eyes sparked in the semi-darkness. I nearly pissed myself. Nothing cut me like a scowl from the man I admired most.

The father bent over his son, kissed his beloved's forehead, and then set fire to the wood under the boat. The villagers threw in their own torches, acting as if nothing was wrong.

Eldgrim signaled me when he judged the flames had reached their zenith. I shook the confusion and worry from my mind and approached the burning boat, said my words clearly and loudly so that all those present could hear, and then dumped the blood into the roaring fire.

The boy's body flaked and seemed to jiggle in the flames. He was not much older than me, perhaps seventeen. His short beard glowed red, and his eyeballs were already boiling.

I turned away.

As I did so, Eldgrim approached and tossed seeds of henbane into the fire.

"Keep your wits," he hissed. And then such words as I'd never heard him speak before: "I prophesize that one day you'll be a greater priest than me."

I stepped back, my tongue tied and tears in my eyes. Why had he chosen to say that at such a moment, amid the ceremony, himself now breaking the sacred rules he had taught me?

Eldgrim lifted his staff and plunged it to the ground. He did this nine times.

A wind from the nearby sea buffeted us. Smoke, now laced with henbane, sluiced the crowd. Everyone, excluding Eldgrim and myself, wailed and beat their chests. They begged the gods' beneficence. The father ran in circles around the boat. "My baby boy!" he cried again and again.

My brain went woozy.

The father ran faster and faster around the burning boat. He ran too fast. He became a dark whirlwind, circling the boat in a blur, like a stone tied to a string and twirled.

I turned to Eldgrim. He nodded at me. Suddenly his mouth and nose and eyebrows disappeared, and his blue eyes stretched until they encompassed his entire face. *I'm hallucinating*, I told myself, refusing to give way to panic. *It's just the henbane.* Eldgrim's eyes peered at me, huge and alien and sad and pompous.

The father still ran around the now-collapsing boat as it gushed embers into the night. But his movements were slow. It made no sense. His legs were extended and his arms swinging as though running at full speed, but his legs bent and fell with incremental slowness. I sought out Eldgrim, who had shifted a few paces away. In the firelight I noticed his green neck tattoo was covered with curly white hair. This was odd. Eldgrim thought it his priestly duty to shave his cheeks and neck before any ship burial. His white cloak was the same. His bronze staff was the same. The form of the man, strong and broad-shouldered with a graceful little paunch that nevertheless seemed muscular—that was all the same. But this man before me had a bushy white beard and bald head.

The priest who wasn't Eldgrim smiled at me at the usual human speed, despite the slow-running father in my periphery. This priest's eyes were amber—not the sparkling blue I so feared.

I had to get a grip. I called on our goddess, the near-forgotten Modgud, the maiden guarding the bridge over the river of the dead, to steady my nerves. I had attended to perhaps twenty ceremonies but never had the henbane affected me so. I felt like my brain was leaking from my ears. It was horrible, humiliating. Even in my unstable frame of mind, I retained enough discipline to not cry out and disturb the grief of the father and villagers. Eldgrim always insisted on utter propriety.

The priest who was not Eldgrim approached me.

"I'm sorry for your loss," he whispered. He winked at me and then all went dark.

ᘓ

In my dream, I asked Eldgrim for the secret words that would make me a priest. Only a teacher can bestow these words upon a pupil, and the set of words is always unique and unguessable.

Eldgrim had grown far thinner, almost like a mummy, but his voice rang clearly as always.

"You were an agreeable and devoted apprentice," Eldgrim said. "Not the smartest of my pupils. But you've improved at an astonishing rate. What you lack in talent you've made up for with commitment and perseverance. I've grown to respect this about you."

"Thank you," I said uncertainly, a little offended. "But these aren't the secret words. You said I am meant to become a greater priest than you. And to be a priest, I must know the words."

"You don't think I understand this, Gizur? What do you take me for?"

I quailed. "Of course. I'm sorry. But then...how am I to become a priest if you're lost to me?"

"Who said I'm lost to you?"

"But that white-bearded priest changed places with you."

"Again, listen when I speak—who said I'm lost to you?"

I awoke at dawn. The priest who was not Eldgrim sat beside the burial mound that had been erected over the ashes of the boy and his boat. It was covered with moss as if it had stood there for a hundred years. How had such a construction been accomplished in one night? Neither the father nor the villagers were present. It had stopped snowing, and the horizon smoked with faint grey light.

No evidence of last night's ceremony remained: no animal corpses or blood or charred wood could be seen anywhere. I was still groggy, trying to master my wits. The bushy-bearded stranger in my teacher's clothing gazed at me curiously. Part of me wanted to attack this imposter—but perhaps there was some rational explanation that the henbane's fumes had withheld from me.

"Where's Eldgrim?" I asked. "One moment he was here and the next gone."

"Is that his name?" the stranger muttered.

"Where is he?"

The bushy-bearded priest cast his eyes to the heavens. "Only Odin knows."

"What do you mean?" I demanded. My anger started to boil.

"Easy, son," he said. "This is all my fault, but I don't know how to fix it. I'm a broken man, you see. King Harald took everything from me and my family and ravaged my village. I resisted with arms, and they sentenced me to the gallows. As the rope was being knotted, I beseeched the All-Father to send me to another land, to take the place of some more fortunate man. I closed my eyes; and when I opened them, I had been transported here in these clothes not so different from my own priestly robes, with an unknown apprentice at my side."

I backed away a little.

"Impossible."

"Then you lack faith," the priest said.

Modgud, give me strength, ease my heart, calm my fury, I thought. I took a deep breath. "If this is true," I said, "you seem unconcerned about my teacher. He's a great man; few on this earth have ever had such an intellect and connection with a god. His prayers are almost always answered. The gods would not disfavor him so. Where do you think he's gone? Not to Valhalla?"

"It's in the gods' hands," the priest said.

I jumped up and pushed him over. I couldn't help it. The priest, crumpled on the moss, chuckled sadly.

"You'll harm an old man? What glory is in that? I made a rash choice; I can't say I'm sorry for it. I wasn't ready to die. Maybe there are deeds of honor left for me to perform after all."

"I'm lost without Eldgrim," I said. "I'm not even a priest yet."

"I cannot give you your secret words."

"I didn't ask you for that," I snapped. "A real priest would've been ready to die when his time came. Have you no council for me, coward?"

"I wish I had. Truly. I'm sorry for you. Maybe Eldgrim is back at his farm? I don't know how the gods manage these exchanges—I hope he did not meet his end on the gallows intended for me. I cannot help you. I must figure out my own situation, where to go in this land, where to make my mark. Have you any advice for me, apprentice? Where should I go?"

"Straight into the ocean," I said. "It's not far from here."

With that, I struck off towards the farm. Maybe Eldgrim was there after all.

ଓ

Eldgrim owned a farm three valleys away, but given the size of the mountains, the journey took two days on horseback. The farm was called Lokhilla and I had lived there for three years with Eldgrim and two farmhands, Hundi the Scot and a former Viking named Ketill (my luckless, loveless parents, who now lived in Orkney, bartered my apprenticeship to Eldgrim for a boat's worth of timber). Lokhilla lay by a small lake, full of fish, and consisted of three buildings and a small temple to Modgud.

Hundi, to whom I was closest—Ketill tended to be grim and silent—told me that Eldgrim had not come home. He was disturbed by my news and desired to assist in my search, but I asked him to stay with the sheep and guard the farm so that no greedy outlaw got any ideas.

"I won't be gone long, I'm sure," I said. "Just keep an eye out for anything untoward. Something's wrong with the world right now. I sense it. But I vow to find Eldgrim."

"Be on your guard," Hundi said. "This is some trick or test or I don't know what. If the gods are involved, you must be extra careful. But where will you go?"

"I don't know," I admitted. "I have no idea, actually. Where should I start?"

He thought for a moment. "I'd go to the witch in Krakaness Forest. What's her name? Ylg? That's it. I've heard she often gives council to the needy—though it isn't always to their benefit. Make sure she sees you as canny and intelligent. I've heard she's vicious to the witless. I don't have to tell you that witches are dangerous and your intestines could end up on a divination cloth."

"Krakaness Forest is to the north, yes?" I said, ignoring his warnings; I was well aware of the dangers of witches.

"Almost directly north. But remember the rest."

"Very good," I said, embracing Hundi. "Make sacrifices to Modgud in our stead. And burn the owl's pellets."

"My best will have to do since I haven't memorized the ceremony. I'm no priest."

"That's enough. Just think of Modgud and us and all will be well."

Hundi embraced me again and helped me fill a sack with dried cod. I prepared my horse, Drott.

I rode north through the cold, winding valleys, whose trees were shagged with a snowfall we didn't experience farther south. In the brief daylight of the second day, lightning struck all around me, the thunder reverberating through my body. I stopped at lonely farmhouses to inquire about Eldgrim, but even though many knew him, none had seen him for months.

I passed a tree that had clearly acted as a gallows but saw no body and no burial mound. Nearby a village burned. My search of the area came up empty. I prayed that Eldgrim did not meet his end on a noose.

Aspens clicked yellow leaves and ptarmigans exploded across my path. Reindeer in rut clashed magnificent antlers. I refused to sleep more than a few hours and always did so in the saddle instead of dismounting. After three days, Krakaness Forest bristled from a mountainside. I was freezing and exhausted yet hopeful. Priests understand witches better than the common farmer or warrior. Her riddles would be far less mysterious to me.

My horse deserved a rest, and I let him roam the rusty shrubland just outside the forest. Though it was midday, darkness swallowed me when I entered the towering spruces. Mushrooms squelched under my feet. Modgud, I am certain, led me in the right direction, on an invisible bridge of her own making, to a little hill with a wooden door in it. Above, in the high branches, shadowy figures swung from ropes—I counted nine in all and understood them to be human sacrifices to the gods. The branches creaked loudly. There was no scent of death, however; the smell of crushed basil leaves pervaded the air.

I bowed before the hillock.

"Ylg!" I cried. "Witch of Krakaness Forest! I bow before your temple." I took out a knife and cut my finger and let the blood drip on the soil. "This blood offering to the cult of your god I offer with all humility."

The door in the hillside creaked open.

A face leaned out of the darkness. Backgrounded by candlelight, it seemed to hover then drift to the ground.

"Crawl," Ylg said. "Crawl to me."

It's a test, I thought. *Show your mettle and make Eldgrim proud.*

I crawled a few paces. The head in the doorway, with black hair hiding the face, glided along the ground and was not connected to any neck I could see. It bobbed up and down as though the witch were swimming through the earth, with only the head breaking the surface—yet no earth shifted beneath her. I nearly fainted with fear. It felt like a hundred shields sat on my back, but somehow I kept crawling, knowing that to refuse a witch's command would have terrible consequences. The mass of black hair inched forward until we were a few feet apart.

"What do you seek, apprentice?" she asked hoarsely. The hair hiding her mouth did not puff outward with breath. It hung there, motionless.

"Eldgrim," I whispered.

Above us, the branches creaked with the hanging people.

"You seek the words to make you a priest?" Ylg asked.

"I seek Eldgrim first, the words second."

"Why do you love him so? Tell me."

I spoke automatically, too afraid to think.

"Because he scared me into being a better, stronger person. He taught me to love the history of the gods. He showed me Modgud's secret paths, took me in his arms and led me to the bridge of Hel. I have seen worlds because of him. He's the man I want to be and was a father to me."

"You speak truly," Ylg said. "Now reach into my hair, right where you think my eyes should be."

"What will I find?" I asked, sickening at the thought.

"Pass the veil of my hair and you will find an item to guide you on your journey."

I lay down so that my head was on the same level as hers. I could see no face beyond the black hair. Hesitantly, I reached forward. My fingertips parted the strands, yet I could still detect no skin behind it—only more hair. I bit my lip as my fingers touched her slick eyeball.

"And you want me to do what?"

"Pluck it out," she said.

"The eyeball?"

"What else, apprentice?"

I gulped. I squeezed the slimy eyeball with my fingers. I yanked it out quickly and it made a popping noise. The witch did not react. The eyeball in my palm was very light and pale as a fish bladder.

"The other eye was eaten by flies long ago," she said. "Flies sent by the trickster god, whom I refuse to name. If you'd chosen the wrong eye, apprentice, and thrust that dirty finger of yours into my hollow socket, your neck would be noosed and bending a branch right now."

"I'm glad I didn't know that," I said.

"Now swallow it whole. No chewing."

"The eye?" I asked, not believing what I'd heard.

"What else?" Ylg said, her hair still a black, frozen waterfall unruffled by breath. "Swallow it whole and gently. If your teeth touch it, you die. Now hurry. I've things to do."

I did as she commanded. I winced, but surprisingly, the eyeball tasted good, like basil and smoked meat.

When the eyeball slid into my stomach and anchored there, I experienced a vision.

I found myself on a snowy plain on a cloudless blue day. Before me ran a river, but rather than the soft gurgle of water, there was an earsplitting clanging and screeching. I stood up and walked forward. The river was very wide. Yet the dancing silver wasn't water. There was no water to speak of. This was a river of weapons, of swords tumbling over each other, their metal glinting in the sunlight.

Across this river of weapons, perhaps a hundred paces away, stood a naked man, emaciated, his ribs flaring, covered in cuts and welts as though he'd been dragged by horses. His features were difficult to make out at first, especially with all the somersaulting iron sending light into my eyes. But then, between the flashes, two dazzlingly blue eyes glittered. The shoulders were broad despite the man's brutal thinness.

It was Eldgrim.

He shouted words at me, but I couldn't hear them. He knocked his knuckles against his head, code for me to think, that I wasn't using all my brain's resources. I took another step toward the waves of swords. I stuck out my foot. He shook his head and kept shouting, presumably the secret words that would endow me with priesthood. It was tantalizing, infuriating.

The vision ended.

I had a bowel movement, passing the witch's eye. I didn't know where I was or what I was doing, but I could feel that gelatinous eye leaving my system. When I came to, I lay outside Krakaness Forest and my horse, Drott, was licking my cheek. I made my way to a nearby creek, washed myself and my clothes, and rode farther north, pondering the vision given to me by the witch and not daring to enter that forest again.

☙

A river of weapons. What did it mean? The dream hummed with significance.

In my vision, the snow by the river of weapons had been knee-deep, as if it lay much farther north.

I asked every person I encountered about a lost or wandering priest of Modgud. No one had seen such a man. Many in this country had not even heard of our goddess.

Poor, ignorant souls, worshipping Odin, Thor, and Frey, whose divine minds are overfull of human prayers, who have enough to do without responding to every stick of incense lit and every bowl of blood spilled at their altars. No deity, even the greatest, is all-powerful. You must have some sympathy for the gods, too, as Eldgrim taught me; the near-forgotten gods are the best to worship and the most loyal friends because they have more time to listen to prayers and ponder their subjects' fates.

One night, halfway up a mountain, I joined the bonfire of a poet who had been ousted from King Harald's Hall. Her name was Osk; she had golden hair and scars on her face as though she'd been a warrior in times past.

For a while we stared into the fire silently. Then I worked up the courage and told her of my plight.

"A river of swords?" she said. "I don't know if I'm the best interpreter of dreams; the gods have not blessed me with poetic inspiration as of late. I've been on a streak of bad luck, so I hesitate to give council. But I'll say this. A river of swords, in the poems of skalds, often refers to a battle, a heated battle between bitter enemies, where the two forces' iron is likened to a river. It could be a kenning, a kind of metaphor. Perhaps you have to seek a battle to find your goal."

She wished me luck, and we went to sleep. When I awoke at twilight, Osk was gone.

I skirted along a fjord for a day; a whale breached the water and crashed down. At a small settlement with a rocky beach, I partook of mead and fresh mackerel. As I ate, it started snowing and didn't look to let up, so I decided to spend the night in the guest house of a well-to-do fisherman who liked to put up guests, believing Odin would honor him for it.

There I met another traveler, a man who called himself Ulfar the Godless. I also told him of my plight. He had a black beard and was very handsome. I was somewhat envious of his good looks.

"Now don't be offended, friend," he said. "Let me show you something." He brought his fist down on the table and rolled his eyes to the heavens. "A curse on Odin, a curse on Thor and Frey and Freya and Heimdall and Loki and the whole lot of them. If they exist, strike me dead."

This Ulfar was a madman. I backed away from him.

"The gods will return this taunt openly or secretly," I scolded. "It's one thing to prefer one god to another—but this blasphemy will send many evils your way. Be careful what you say."

"Here's my point," Ulfar said. "I know it will offend you. Forgive me. But I have been given second sight and know that the gods are dead. The one you worship, Modgud, is a corpse or a fantasy. Don't waste your time with her. I see that you want to strike me. Go ahead and do it—Modgud certainly won't harm me. If the gods existed, one of them would have punished me by now. I do this to save you pain. The life of a priest is barren. You can rely on nothing but your own strength and luck. Sacrifices are pointless; nothing is sacred but your own brief life. Go back to your farm and seek your teacher there. I'm sure there's a sensible explanation for all this."

I had been hesitating between striking him and fleeing the entire time. How could someone be so blind? How could a man be stranded on such a far-off plane of reality?

In the end, I gathered my things and slept on the floor of a poor fisherman's hut, safe from Ulfar's dark words. I would not let his atheism affect me; I would remain steadfast.

☙

Days later, a soothsayer, casting chips onto a cloth, told me an earl's war party was heading north; the earl had refused to submit to Harald Fairhair and went to meet a large force of the king's army on the battlefield. This was the sign I'd been seeking. If the poet Osk was correct, and a river of swords did in fact mean a battle, then perhaps I would find my teacher at long last.

I journeyed into a land where some say giants roam. Doubts still plagued me despite my resolve to smother them. Had my visions been mere fantasies? Had the poet Osk given me an incorrect interpretation of the river of swords? Was my faith in Modgud strong enough? Eldgrim might have been wrong about my future priesthood—something I'd never considered before, strange as that may sound. Eldgrim penetrated deeply into things; I'd never known him to make an inaccurate prediction. Maybe I was even more talentless than he had supposed and my perseverance, which he claimed to admire, was far more brittle. The thought that I had fended off for so long—that I was chasing a ghost—started to bend my resolve to the breaking point. My horse fell deeper and deeper into the snow.

When I was about to turn Drott around, I came across a battlefield.

A river of swords? Certainly not: it was an inactive battlefield. Hundreds of men lay still, their armor glistening with frost. Shields had been cloven, helmets dented and cracked, arms and feet and heads and fingers severed. Beards blossomed with gore and eyes stared blankly at the sky. Yet amid this field of slaughter—which I supposed to be the aftermath of King Harald's victory over the recalcitrant earl—two creatures still fought. As I parted a wall of mist, I saw something that unsettled my mind and made me wonder, once again, what had happened to the world I'd once known. Before me, two horses, one white and the other dapple gray, battled viciously. They frothed at the mouth and clamped down on each other's necks, tearing away flesh. Yet not only did they bite and wound each other—they swallowed the morsels they'd torn away. They lifted their necks and gulped before again charging their adversary with manes flying and teeth bared. I yelled and tried to intervene, but Drott would not take a step nearer the blood-soaked steeds, and I feared something unearthly was at stake in this battle between them.

☙

Severely rattled, I turned my horse to the south. I'd failed. I'd never find Eldgrim or learn the words to make me a priest. Modgud did not love me, and all prophecies had failed. My thoughts buzzed, and for many hours I did not even note the landscapes I passed by. It snowed, but I hardly felt it. If it weren't for Drott, whom I had to care for, I would have slumped off the saddle, fallen into a drift, and allowed the cold to take me. I'd always heard that freezing to death was the sweetest, gentlest way to pass to the other world. No one but Hundi would miss me.

The brief snowstorm ceased. I shook off my despair for a moment and looked around. I didn't recognize this land—I hadn't ridden through it earlier. I was totally lost.

Then I heard something: axes grinding? Another battle? As I neared the sounds, they grew more chaotic and cacophonous. I debated veering off in another direction. Suddenly, it came to me. This was the place. No mountains serrated the horizon. The sun blazed much too fiercely for late autumn.

I had emerged onto a snowy plain and before me ran a river.

The silver water—or rather the silver blades—danced as they had in my vision. The river of swords was no metaphor; it was an actual phenomenon. For all I knew, the strange battlefield had been a conduit to this spot, a necessary stepping stone. Part of me wanted to hoot for joy, but the fear of the metallic river, flowing with its razor-sharp weapons—the very sublimity of it all—tempered my happiness. And though my love of Modgud burned brighter than ever, I felt ashamed, too, for I had doubted her wisdom in guiding devout wanderers to their goal.

Was *he* here? Despite my fear and shame, I hastened forward. Did Eldgrim stand beyond the river? Was my teacher and foster father alive? Sharing a mead with him, something as small as that, would reduce me to tears. When drunk, Eldgrim's harshness melted, his keen eyes softened, and he would bellow full-belly laughter at any quip. Beyond his stony mask lay real decency.

An infinity of swords surged from east to west as far as the eye could see. They clashed and shrieked, tumbling over invisible rocks, leaping into the air like demented fish. Were they weapons flowing from Valhalla, those of all the warriors who had ever died in combat? I dismounted and approached this river of death cautiously. I blinked through the sunlight, searching for Eldgrim on the other side. No bridge arced over the river. The riddle of crossing it was meant for me to solve.

In my vision, Eldgrim had shouted at me from the far side of the river. Yet he was still nowhere in sight.

"Eldgrim!" I yelled. "Eldgrim, I'm here!"

No answer.

I closed my eyes and pictured Modgud guarding Hel's bridge, under which the fiery green waters of Gjöll swirled. Modgud stood helmeted with a spear in hand, a giant among the gods. Her hair was white yet her face ageless. Her eyes were big pupil-less globes of blood.

I held my foot over the scissoring blades and set it down on something hard and smooth. A stone? Indeed: a single stone lay atop the river of swords, held in place by what, I couldn't say. Modgud would ease my passage. Here was the first stone of a bridge across the river of swords. I need not fear anymore. I lifted my foot again with renewed confidence, but as I lowered it, expecting to meet another stone, a sword sprung up and pierced it; for a moment I felt only confusion, then the searing pain began. I howled, clasping my sword-pierced foot. Why would Modgud give with one hand and take away with the other? I took a deep breath, grabbed the hilt, and withdrew the sword from my flesh, little stray bones crinkling and tendons stretching as the skin puckered outward. All the while, of course, I screamed. Once done, I tossed the sword back into the current. The wound was evil, festering.

"Eldgrim," I cried again. "Help me! Tell me what to do, how to speak to Modgud! I lack your gifts. Please, wherever you are, help me!"

Of course, no answer.

I was to be a greater priest than him. He'd said that.

A greater priest. Not a better? Not a wiser? Was there a distinction? He always used words in such particular ways, each one accruing complex shades of meaning.

An inspiration, whether divine or otherwise, hit me.

Perhaps Eldgrim meant something different than I had supposed. I could never worship Modgud with the same enthusiasm and originality as he had. He had practically discovered half of her cult through disembodied meetings with her on the bridge Gjallarbrú and through whispered consultations with his mouth to the earth. On many occasions I had pressed my ear to the ground to hear Modgud's voice as he had instructed, but I had never heard it clearly—only garbled murmurings. Maybe Eldgrim meant that I'd be greater in that I would cut a broader swath, make sacrifices to *all* the gods, not just one, and rise to the challenge of a vibrant polytheism. While my worship would be less refined, I could attend to the cults of each god equally. Eldgrim was a specialist. I could seek variety. Each god would offer me a pittance of favor, yet a pittance from every god would amass great spiritual wealth.

"Heimdall!" I cried. "Guardian of the rainbow bridge, brother of Modgud, I call on you for aid!"

I set my injured foot down, barely able to stand on it, but this time it met another stone.

"Odin!" I cried.

Another stone appeared across the river of swords.

"Frey!" I cried.

Another stone of the bridge appeared.

I called on Freya and Thor and Frigg and Loki and Idunn and Delling and Hel and Höthr and Tyr and Skathi and Njord and Mimir and Hœnir and Baldur and Forseti and Sol and Vali and Andhrimnir and on and on. With the name of each god of the pantheon, a stone materialized.

On Eldgrim's farm, I would build small temples for all the Æsir and Vanir, a truly grand undertaking, and worship their graven images daily.

Soon I'd limped across the entire bridge and alighted on the opposite bank. I twisted this way and that, seeking Eldgrim in the snow, which was a mere dusting on this side of the river. Where was his emaciated body with flaring ribs, as I'd seen in the vision?

"Crawl!" a hoarse voice cried. "Crawl to me!"

I dropped down and crawled forward, my heart fluttering, believing this voice to be Eldgrim's. I didn't stop until pain shot through one of my fingertips; it felt like it had been bitten.

"Stop!" Eldgrim said. It was his voice but veiled with exhaustion.

He was nowhere in sight.

"Down," he said.

In the snow was a wide-open mouth. A tongue fluttered between squarish teeth. Eldgrim's teeth, unmistakably.

"All of my body has been transported to Valhalla," Eldgrim said, "except my mouth. I left that here for you, to give you your words. You've earned them and you've made me proud. You cannot be what I was; you can be both less and more. Now thrive, my pupil."

"Eldgrim," I said, "it's too much. I don't know what to say."

The white teeth clicked together, and the lips spread into a smile.

"I suppose you're speaking now but I can't hear you. I told you: nothing's left of me on this plane except my mouth. Don't be dim and ask me to come home with you. My farm's yours now, Gizur."

"I love you," I said. "Because of your severity, I've seen myself more clearly."

There was silence.

"Well, what're you waiting for?" Eldgrim said. "Hurry up and retrieve your words. Become a priest. Valhalla's little fun without drinking and I'd like to converse with a few poets and kings and fellow priests at the mead benches. It's time for this mouth to die, too."

"Goodbye," I said. "I won't forget you."

I knew what I had to do.

I reached into the mouth in the snow, spreading it wide, splitting the upper and lower lips. Teeth scraped the sides of my hand, and my fingers passed the uvula. I reached down until I clasped something glittering. And when I pulled out my hand, it was overflowing with beautiful words.

ACKNOWLEDGMENTS

I would like to thank my partner, Jessica Fordham Kidd, for her endless support, kindness, wisdom, and humor; my parents and sister for their unshakable love and generosity; Marc Jolley for championing unconventional projects; Sara Pirkle for pointing me to Mercer University Press; James Hutton and Aleksandra Apocalisse for their brilliant, inspired illustrations; and the friends who read drafts of some of these stories and gave thoughtful feedback: Matthew Oglesby, Katherine Packert Burke, and Robert Gwaltney, among others. Also, a thousand thanks to my friends who make me laugh and tolerate my eccentricities: Michael Xu, Isaac Solomon, Shakera Solomon, Shane McKeen, John Alves, Kartik Patel, Ian Volpi, Cecilia Piantanida, and Emrys Donaldson.